Books by

Blind Ride

ISBN # 978-1-78651-896-5

©Copyright BA Tortuga 2016

Cover Art by Posh Gosh ©Copyright 2016

Interior text design by Claire Siemaszkiewicz

Pride Publishing

Published in 2016 by Pride Publishing, Newland House, The Point, Weaver Road, Lincoln, LN6 3QN, United Kingdom.

Pride Publishing is a subsidiary of Totally Entwined Group Limited.

Printed in Great Britain by Clays Ltd, St Ives plc

1

Roughstock

BLIND RIDE

BA TORTUGA

Dedication

To every Texan reader who ever looked at me and said,
"You wrote my home."
Bless y'all. I try.

Chapter One

Jason stood there with the big fake check for the event win, watching the crowd go one of two ways—up and out of the stands, or down to wait for the guys to make the autograph circuit. He fucking hated this part.

That little broad from the XSports channel was waiting with her bright orange hair and her too tight jeans. He knew how it'd go, too. *Blah blah blah Jason Scott blah blah blah race for the finals blah blah blah new kids chasing his ass.*

Goodie.

He managed to get through all the questions without being an asshole, but not before a huge stack of fans were hanging over the fence, waving programs and hats, hollering his name. He ducked under into the pens and headed toward the back. He just wasn't good at that whole meet-and-greet thing.

"You're gonna get a reputation as an asshole, man." His best buddy, Andy Baxter, fell in beside him, boots clacking against the concrete walkway back to the locker room.

"Yeah, yeah. Better let them think I might be than know I am. 'sides, I don't see your happy ass out there, Bax."

And shit, nine times out of ten Bax was out there glad-handing.

"It was a long night. My knee's killin' me."

That slow Texas drawl always made him smile, because it made everyone think Bax was laid-back, maybe not so bright.

Jason knew better.

"Yeah?" He winced, shook his head. "You came down on it fucking hard. I swear that bull has it out for you."

5

It was hell getting old.

"I did." Bax shrugged, sticking his hands in the pockets of his old school Wranglers. "I ain't the man of steel I used to be."

"Bullshit." There wasn't any bastard on Earth tough as Bax. He knew it to the bone. "You want to go get a steak?"

"Hell, yes. Someplace not at the hotel." They were staying at the sanctioned hotel because the sponsors had asked Jason to, but eating there was like sitting in a fishbowl.

"I got the truck here. We can go anywhere." He nodded to Little Jack and Harvey who were still waiting outside sports medicine. DJ had taken one hell of a spill, just got caught up and dragged. "Y'all heard something?"

Jack shook his head. "They ain't called the am'blance. That's gotta be good, huh?"

"I guess."

"Well, you call me, you hear something, yeah?" Bax said, nodding. "Come on, man. Food."

"I hear you, old man." He winked at Jack, headed off, following that tight little ass to get their gear.

"Not that much older than you, Mini." Bax took every opportunity to give him shit about how much shorter he was.

"Three years is a fucking eternity." He ducked the lazy swing, just hooting with it. "You still scattered from the round, man? You missed."

"You were on the move. Stand up and let me hit you, man." That laugh was sure enough the best way to make him forget all the shit his sponsors wished he would do.

"Fuck you." He started stripping off his shirt, hunting something clean and less dusty.

"Here." One of his hanging shirts landed on his shoulder. "That one looks good on."

"Thanks." He redid the smell-good, the deodorant. Then he changed his boots. "Man, I need a beer."

"We can have that with supper. Or, hey, we could go play some pool." Oh, yeah, because Bax wanted to shark that five thousand he'd won in the second go-round.

"We could do both. Hell, after a steak, I might feel ten years younger." He got himself put together, tucked in his shirt and got his belt buckled. Okay. Wallet. Phone. Bag. Time to get out of Dodge. "Besides, all the buckle bunnies'll be gone home by late."

"True enough." They went out the back way, Bax's white shirt setting off his deep tan, that black hat playing hide and seek with Bax's dark brown eyes and smile lines.

Jason tossed his gear into the back, thumping his cock but good as it did its dead-level best to wake up and say hello and howdy to Bax.

Good night. You'd think he was a Brazilian after a good ride. *Down boy.*

Bax threw his duffel back, too, sliding into the driver's side. "So, where to? I figure that one little place where you circle your order will be closed."

"There's that one place by the highway — about twenty minutes out. It's nothing but old ranchers taking their women out. Nice T-bones." And he always got tickled by those tables with the ads printed on them. Reminded him of going to auction with Pa-paw.

"That works." The big dualie slid into traffic like an elephant into a herd of zebras, Bax muscling them right in.

They scooted down 35, radio blaring. He found a pack of smokes in the console and lit one for Bax, then got himself one. Three days of rest, then Tulsa.

"You think we ought to try and hit home 'fore Tulsa?"

It was kinda eerie sometimes, the way Bax read his mind. Then again, they'd been on the road together for nigh on six years.

"We can. Momma'd like to see us. 'Course, we could go on to the city. Goof off. Depends on how much you want Momma's pineapple upside down cake."

"Oh, I'd rather go see your momma." That man did have a sweet tooth. Pineapple upside down was Bax's very favorite.

"Cool. I'll call her. Let her know we'll be in." He took a deep drag, grinned. *Lord, lord.* "I hope your knee's up to riding fence."

"Shit, you know it. Just don't ask me to walk fence." Wheeling around a little Honda, Bax started humming with George on the radio, off tune as anything.

"Nah. You wouldn't be worth shit in Tulsa, then."

They both hooted, and Jason leaned back, easy in his bones.

Man, event win number three. Check in his pocket. Him and Bax heading for steak.

Life, she was good.

Chapter Two

Damn, life was good.

Bax liked riding fence. Well, all right, if he was honest, he liked riding fence with Jason. Somewhere after the first hour, Jason would take that starched shirt off and tie it to the back of the saddle, leaving him in just a tight, white undershirt, and damn. Oh, damn, Bax loved that.

Licking sweat off his upper lip, Bax leaned down to check a post joint, grinning when it wasn't as dry rotted as he'd thought. "You think your momma's baking right now?"

"Yup. She's making a pie and one of them cakes you like. I saw beans on the back of the stove, so it'll be brisket and cornbread for dinner." Mini's momma was as predictable as the day was long and, lord, that woman loved to cook.

"Oh, you know I like that." Damn, his knee was throbbing. He pulled his bad leg up, leaning back in the saddle and stretching it out.

"You need to walk some, man?" Jason rode up closer, horses touching noses as Mini reached out, touched his knee. "It's pretty swolled."

The feel of that hand on him made him jump, even through work glove and jeans. "Nah. I'm good. I just need to remember not to lean so hard on the stirrup.

"'Kay." He was given one more stroke—the crookedy thumb on Jason's riding hand rubbing the inside a bit.

His cheeks heated up, and he was damned glad of the sun. Long as they'd been riding together, Bax'd never told Jason a bit what the man could do to him with just a touch.

"Anyway, we ain't got much more to do today."

"Nope. You want to ride to the river? Swim?" That straw

hat was pushed back, the collar of Jason's T-shirt wet with sweat.

"Shit, yes." That water would be like bathwater, but it would be so damned nice to get wet. Bax approved. "Come on, slowpoke."

"Slow... Oh, you old bastard!" Jason whomped Heidi, the two going tearing across the pasture, ass tight as a boar's backside in that saddle.

Bax sat there for a full five seconds with his teeth in his mouth. Then he whooped and spurred and he was off, too, Little Bit happy to be heading for the river and giving it some speed.

It did him a world of good, just to flat-out run, to lean down and let the bullshit go. Jason was feeling it, too, the constant fucking pressure, the need to keep on his game. It made shit like this more and more important.

Lord love him, they both loved what they did, but it was getting more and more commercial and... *Jesus, fuck, look at that man ride. Just look.*

"Come on, Bax. That water's waiting on your scarred-up ass."

"Yeah. It's waiting for the water, too." He nudged Bit a little closer before sliding down and ground tying her easy as you please. Bax groaned, his leg stiff as a board.

"Here. Let me loosen it up. There ain't no one here to point and say you're getting old but me." Then Jason knelt, hands on his leg, just working his bum knee.

Staring down at that bent head, Bax thought about Heaven, and how it might be just like this. Of course, if he started entertaining fantasies about what should happen next, it could get some embarrassing. "Thanks, buddy."

"I know it's gotta be sore as a boil." *Fuck.* Fuck, he could feel Jason's breath on his thigh, on his knee.

"It's pretty hot..." His voice sounded like sandpaper. *Christ on a pogo stick.*

"Yeah. I can feel it. You gotta rest it some." The back of Jason's neck was red, a nice deep, dark red.

Bax cleared his throat. "Not till I get that swim in. Come on, man, or we'll miss supper…"

"Yeah. Yeah, sure." Jason scooted back, stood up, and headed toward the bank, bending to tug off his boots.

That ass was enough to give a man palpitations. Hadn't he seen thousands of female heads turn to watch it go by? Turning his back, Bax worked one boot off, but couldn't get the other.

"Goddamn it, Jason. Can you help me with this?"

"Yup." Jason chuckled, bent down again and grabbed his heel. "Pull, old man."

He pulled, his knee creaking, all but going ass over teakettle. Jason's shoulders felt right and tight under his hands when he caught himself and tried to balance.

"There you go." Jason looked up, that mouth just right where he'd like it to be.

Blinking, Bax nodded. "Yup. There you go. Thanks." All he could do was stand there and stare, one foot up like a stork or something.

"Uh-huh." Jason didn't move for a long second, just took a deep, deep breath.

Finally Bax moved, putting his foot down carefully on the prickly ground and backing off. "You going in wearing your jeans?" he asked, going for teasing and almost making it.

"Nah, they'll chafe riding home." Jason stood, giving him a peek at something full and hard in those Wranglers. A quick thump and a grunt and Jason started working them off.

Oh. Oh, Lord. Curse him for a coward, but he just didn't have the gumption to reach for that. Bax wanted to. He sure as Hell did. But he didn't want to ruin nothin'. He gave his own crotch a good whack and got to getting naked.

Jason draped jeans and T-shirt over some brush and waded in, nothing but that beat-up hat on. Fuck him, that was fine. Even with the bruises and the so-pale-it-glowed ass, Jason was the prettiest thing he'd ever seen. Bax got

11

bare and slid on down the bank, the water feeling slick and cool on his skin.

"That better on your knee, Bax?" Jason leaned back, moving lazily, just keeping his hat brim out of the water.

"Shit, yes. Taking the hurt right out." It was almost like the hot tub at that one hotel that time... Well. They'd both been real drunk, then.

Real drunk. Real happy. Horny as fuck and needing.

It was still his favorite memory to jack off to.

"Good deal. I do love this spot."

"Mmmhmm." His toes popped right up to the surface for a moment, making him hoot before his ass started to sink. "Pretty and peaceful and all..."

"Yup. I used to come out here when I was a kid, spend hours avoiding the chores." Jason's toes wiggled.

"Lazy-ass." There wasn't no 'avoiding chores' at his house. Bax would've gotten his butt beat.

"You know it. Daddy was raising pigs at the time. You ever smelled pigs up close?"

"Yes. Not my idea of a good time." Stink. Lord. Stretching, he groaned happily, arms moving just enough to keep him in place.

"Nope. Big, stinky and meaner than bulls." Jason chuckled, kicked a little. "Not meaner than KC, though. That's a bad-tempered son of a bitch."

That was the God's honest truth. "That's not just mean. That's stone crazy."

"Yeah, well, you grew up looking like an undead monkey, you'd be mean, too."

"Well, you ought to know all about that, you little chimp..." Oh, if Jason connected with that swat it was gonna hurt.

The water took most of the slap, but those fingertips got him but good. *Bastard.*

"Don't make me twist your nipple off, buddy. You'd be all lopsided." He would, too, if he had to.

"I need that for balance, Bax. That titty's worth thousands."

That had him laughing so hard that he all but sank and drowned. "The million dollar boob."

"Yep. Worth a fortune. Not just for decoration."

They both got to laughing, the sound echoing, ringing out.

* * * *

The sun had moved a good ways over in the sky when they finally climbed out of the water, all wrinkly and thankfully not worrying about springing a happy. "I bet your momma has upside down cake by now."

"You know she does. Come on, old man. We'll get fed and then we can drive into town and shoot some pool."

"Sounds good." No one would bother them a bit at home, and he could ogle that sweet ass to his heart's content. Like he was doing now.

13

Chapter Three

"Hey, Momma." Jason hung his hat on the hook, nudging
Stu and Beemer out of the way, hound dog ears flailing as
they fought to get out, to get to Bax. Drooling beasts.

"Hey, boys. Y'all get that fence seen to?"

He grabbed Beemer's collar pulled him off Bax's knee.
"Yeah, Momma."

Nag. Nag. Nag.

"Good. I made y'all cornbread and all. Get the horse off
you. Andy, I put your laundry on your bed." Momma came
bustling through, apron all white with flour and her hair
piled up in a granny knot. Lord. It was quite a look over top
of her Rocky Mountain jeans and her scuffed up old boots.

Bax, who was Andy to every other fool in the world but
him, nodded and grinned and pulled one of Momma's
apron strings. "Thanks. Can I have cake first?"

She swatted his hand but good, snorting. "You cannot.
That's for dessert, son."

Jason cackled, grabbed her by the waist and hauled her
around, the apron going flying. "Rules, rules, rules."

Laughing and beating out a tattoo for them to dance to,
Bax egged him on, "Nothing but rules."

He let her feet touch the ground as he two-stepped her
around, her laugh making him grin.

"Y'all were in the pond, weren't you? You smell like
snake-water."

"Yeah, Momma. Me and Bax got all eat up with the
cottonmouths."

The dogs howled at the very mention of the word, making
them all chuckle. Bax washed up and dried off, nodding at

14

Momma. "What can I do, lady?"

"Set the table. Son, go get the meat off the smoker."

"Yes, Momma." He grabbed a cookie sheet and the meat fork, whistling up the puppers as he went out. Jesus Christ, Momma'd put a side of beef in the damned thing.

They'd be eating beef sandwiches out of mini-fridges for a week.

Time Jason got back in, Bax had the table set, the napkins all mangled because he had tried to fold them like Momma did. Like those stiff old broken up fingers was gonna work that well.

"Martha Stewart you ain't, buddy." He did love them hands, though. The way they touched things.

"Oh, shut up, Mini." There was no heat behind it. Just a flash of those dark eyes and a wicked 'fuck you' grin.

"Yeah. Yeah. You see the size of this meat?" Wait, did that sound dirty?

"Uh... Is that a trick question?" Look at the sun that man had gotten on his cheeks today.

He snorted, damn near choking as he started laughing, the meat sliding on the pan. "Shit. Shit."

"Don't you drop that, son."

"No, ma'am."

Bax came to help him, abandoning the twisted and ripped napkins. "No letting the dogs have our supper."

"I left them outside. Thanks, man." They got it settled on the counter, and Momma handed Bax a carving knife.

"Oh. Duh." While he bustled around grabbing stuff, Bax carved, slicing it nice and thin. "Okay, folks, let's eat."

"Momma, you outdid yourself." Potato salad, coleslaw, bread. Man, it was nice to be home.

Even if it was for just a few days.

Bax grinned. "I can smell that cake."

"I made two little ones. One for tonight, one for y'all's cooler."

"Score!" Bax leaned over and kissed Momma's cheek. "I'm your favorite son, right?"

"You know it."

"Hey!" He kicked Bax's ankle but hard. Asshole. Kissing up on his momma. "Man, a guy can't get a break."

"Sure you can. I can break your foot, Mini." He got a kick right back, as Bax scooped up potatoes.

"Fuckhead."

"Watch your mouth at my table, Jason Patrick Scott."

"Yes, Momma."

Snorting, Bax heaped more food on his plate. "See there? You might be a big star at the arena, but here you're a momma's boy."

"Andy Baxter, you are not too big to be stuck doing the dishes, now. Y'all quit bitchin' and eat."

Jason hid his grin in a bite of slaw. He wasn't the only one Momma could give what for.

"Yes, ma'am." Bax didn't talk to his own mother, so it seemed right somehow that Jason's had taken him on. And she did, too, especially when she thought Bax was being a butthead on TV or something.

They settled right in, eating hearty. He could watch Bax eat for, oh, hours and shit. The man just loved his feed, licking the fork and enjoying every bite and all. Then there were Bax's hands. Lean, tanned dark, and well-shaped, they just fascinated him. They'd been on him so many times while he was in the chute, and he always dreamed of more. He caught himself staring a little, watching those fingers, following the little scars on the back.

Goddamn.

The things he could imagine.

Bax caught him staring finally, dark eyes fastening on his, one eyebrow going up. "You okay, Mini?"

"Yeah. Yeah, just woolgathering, man." *Jesus.*

Just thinking about doing obscene things with you.

"Ready to get on the road already, son?"

"I got two more days, Momma."

"Don't push us out the door, huh?" Bax said, patting her hand. "We need the time off."

"Y'all are welcome home whenever. Two more suppers, huh? Y'all want enchiladas and spaghetti?"

"Oh. Spaghetti. Will you make garlic bread and Italian cream cake?"

Look at that fool man bounce.

"Sure, son, if you and Junior get up on the roof and check shingles."

"Momma, you're evil." He grinned over, winked.

"Shit, Mini, you know I'll do shingles and gutters for that meal." Sometimes it was good to just be home, not be on the road. People figured he and Bax split up to do that, but home was when he enjoyed the man's company the most.

"Yeah. I want to do some maintenance on the tractor." *Maybe take the cutting horses out.*

"And I promised to clean out the old rabbit hutch, yeah?" Bax just worked like a dog.

"You're good boys. Both of you. I bought a bunch of shoot 'em up movies for y'all to watch in the hotels. Oh, and Andy, honey. You need some new shirts. Cain't you get your sponsor to understand that yellow stains?"

"I've tried, Momma." Shrugging easily, Bax just nibbled some more. "They like yellow. It's their logo color."

"It suits you, at least." Momma shook her head, giving him another spoonful of slaw. "Finish that and I won't have to save any."

"Yes, Momma." He nibbled, listening to both of them just jabber on about this and that, the sound familiar as hell. *Shit.*

It was good to be home.

Even if they did have to get on the roof. Luckily they had cake to eat first.

Chapter Four

The crowd was rockin'. Bax loved it when they were into it, cheering and screaming, egging them and the bulls on. It ramped up the energy, made him want to put on a better show. It also made Jason a crazed lunatic. Made the man incredibly determined to cover all his bulls. Bax just loved it.

He stood on the rail, pulling at Jason's rope, watching Mini fold his gloved fingers over and pound on them, getting the rope good and tight in his riding hand.

It was sexy as Hell.

Bax could see Jason clenching his jaw, over and over, knew he was talking to himself, going over the same thing, again and again. Getting ready. The bull was jumpy as fuck, thinking about climbing up and out of the chute, Bax could tell.

Bax crawled over the fence, back behind the chute, snarling, "Give him the nod, for fuck's sake."

"Bitch, bitch, bitch." He got this wild, pure wicked grin and that black hat dipped.

The gate swung open, Triple-Dip jumping strong and going for the right, just like always.

Jesus, that man had balance and grace and pure-D strength. Bax watched every jump and spin, the bull trying to pull Jason forward and missing by a mile. Shit, Mini was spurring, looking as if he was having a ball. Eduardo and Buck were screaming their heads off, AJ pounding Bax on the back as the clock hit eight.

Bax pumped a fist in the air, all but leaping off the gate when the bull turned back and took a swipe at Jason's ass.

He liked that ass in one piece.

Jason took a leap, hanging on the gate, hat going flying as the son of a bitch laughed. "Did you see that, Bax? Did you see that bastard?"

"Fucking A, man." Leaning across, he grabbed Jason's shoulder, laughing like a loon.

The scores came in—89.75. Not bad. Not bad at all. The crowd went wild, Jason waving, grinning wide, heading up and over the chute.

"You'd best go do your interview now or she'll track you down back in the locker room in your skivvies." Bax put an arm around Jason's back a minute, pounding a little.

"That'd show her, huh? Me and my BVDs?" Jason dumped his bull rope, brushed some dust off one cheek. "So, twenty bucks says she wants to know how I feel."

"No bet. She wants to feel you all the time." He winked as AJ hooted and made a rude motion.

"Ew. Bastard." Nasty.

Nas-ty.

The laughter followed Jason out to the cameras, that microphone that got shoved into his face.

"So, Jason, that looked great out there. What is it going to take to win the championship round, do you think?"

Was this woman stupid?

"Uh. I gotta stick on the bull for eight seconds?"

"Jason! Great ride. How do you feel that this affects your ride to the finals?" The chick with the microphone just had this scary, toothy smile.

"It's always good to be healthy and on a streak." Better than being beat to Hell and in a slump.

"Do you think you'll be able to keep the streak going? Kynan Daley is getting closer in the points range." Lord, the questions these people asked over and over.

"Well, assuming I keep riding, I got hope." He could see the guys, down the tunnel, making fun of him.

"Well, good luck. Great ride." She said the same shit, all the time.

"Thanks." Thank fuck. He headed back toward the little pods of pure-D assholes, watching the little fucks scatter.

There was one little boy, waving his cowboy hat madly, eyes huge. "Jason! Mr. Jason! Please!"

Fuck. "Okay. Okay, son."

He grabbed the hat and the pen, signing the brim and handing it back, ignoring the rest.

No more.

He hated glad-handing.

Bax was waiting for him, a big old grin about to split that brown face wide open. "Such charm. Such sophistication."

"Fuck you." He swatted Bax's ass but hard, the sound echoing.

AJ's dorky-assed laugh rang out. "Don't hit it too hard, man. Cooter just barely saved it from Mr. Master today."

"Slowest rider in the league, at least on the ground," Bax agreed cheerfully. "But I got away, huh? Besides, buddy, you need to keep your mind on your own. In the middle." Bax was just that much older than some of them, always mother-henning. You called it mentoring, he might hit you.

"I'm managing. You did some riding today, Cotton. Had all them little girls screaming your name."

The kid went about as red as the hair on his head. Lord, he'd never been that green, had he? "Yeah, well. I... I reckon I'm going back to the hotel and hit the after-party. There's that little blonde..."

"Just make sure the little blonde don't have a big boyfriend." They parted ways after hanging up their ropes, Bax stripping off his vest and cracking his neck. "So. Short go is tomorrow. We're done. You want to sneak out?"

"Yeah. You want to go eat or get something in the room?" Jason got his vest off, rolling his shoulders.

"Sounds good. We could watch some of those movies." They could hide a bit. That was what he could see on Bax's face. The media circus was starting to kind of get to all of them.

"Works for me. We got a cooler full of drinks still. Cards."

He shrugged on a T-shirt, tossed one over to Bax.

"Thanks." After absently yanking off his yellow shirt, Bax pulled the T-shirt on, smoothing it down over that flat belly. "Damn, I got to learn to get off the back instead of the front."

"Least you got off whole." Man, everything that came out of his mouth sounded filthy.

"I did." The riding boots came off, Bax pulling on the old, worn work boots and putting on a gimme cap. "Ready when you are."

He brushed the dust out of his hair and grabbed his straw hat. "Let's blow this popsicle stand, buddy."

He hung back a little, let Bax go first. That way he could watch. The little cowboy ass wiggled as if Bax was showing it just for him. A man could get off on that in a hurry. His prick just got heavy, appreciating the finest sight on this Earth, yessir. The things he could imagine...

"What, am I running interference or something?" That glare was one the camera loved — people loved it when Bax was a bastard. He usually got it when Bax thought he needed to get a move on.

"Jesus Christ, you're the slowest motherfucker on earth when you're in the arena and then, all of the sudden, you're in public and you're fucking Speed Racer?"

"Just trying to get your famous ass past anyone who might be out there, trolling for autographs." When he caught up, Bax grabbed his arm and yanked, kinda like he would pull Jason out of the way of a bull.

"Fuck off, Mr. December." He was never going to let Bax live that shirtless, lying-back-in-the-hay-like-a-slut beefcake calendar picture down. Ever.

"You're just jealous because they didn't ask your skinny ass to be in it."

They made the truck before an old guy in a neon T-shirt figured out if they were who he thought they were, peeling out fast enough that the tires squealed.

"You don't know that they didn't ask." Bax also didn't

know that Jason had that picture in a pocket, all folded up. For when he needed inspiration.

"I do, too. I asked your momma. She reads all your mail, you know." Hooting, Bax floored it and ran a red light, just cackling like a fool.

"Bitch. I hope you get stopped." He propped his feet up on the dashboard, knowing it drove Bax nuts.

"Get your nasty boots off my dash." Like the Dodge wasn't almost six years old, and like Bax had paid any money for it. The lucky fuck had won it at the National Finals Rodeo.

"They ain't nasty. I had 'em polished at the hotel." Man, they were gonna tie it up some, they weren't careful.

'Course, they'd been awful nice of late. Sometimes they just had to bust out, and who better to fly off against? Least they were friends enough not to take it personally.

"You're still gonna scratch it."

"Like I'm not the one who takes it to get detailed." He figured it was the least he could do.

"Well... Man, you're determined to take the starch out of me." Bax sighed, rolled his head on his neck. "I just need a Goddamned ride."

"Yeah. Man, you know slumps happen." But yeah. Yeah, Bax was sliding and Goddamn, he hated that. "You just gotta let it happen, man."

"Aw, Hell, Mini. I'm gettin' old." They streaked around a curve, his elbow and shoulder whacking the window.

"You ain't that old." Only a little older than him. Only enough to prove that he needed to win the big money, have enough to set him up.

"Yeah, well..." They rocked to a stop at the hotel, and thank God there weren't no blue lights following them. "I need a beer."

"Okay. You want to go upstairs or you want the bar?" He sure as shit hoped Mr. Bitchy wasn't wanting to be social.

"Upstairs." Putting those boots down hard, Bax stomped into the hotel, daring anyone to so much as look at him, if that glare meant what it usually did.

"Cute-cute." He rolled his eyes and humped it to the elevators, keeping his head down. Maybe he'd drown the grumpy bastard.

Bax punched their floor and turned on him, growling. "What the fuck is your problem?"

"Looks like you are, man." He could feel his chin jut out, fingers fisting up. "You got a burr under your saddle or do you just need to find some fucking buckle bunny to take the edge off?"

"Buckle bunny... Jesus Christ." Turning back to the doors, Bax clenched his fists and stood there, tense and silent, jaw like steel.

Jason sighed, rubbed the back of his neck. Fuck this shit. He was gonna dump his gear and get the hell out of Dodge. Maybe go shoot some pool. Kick somebody's ass.

The elevator dinged open and they both stepped forward, bumping shoulders but hard. "Goddamn it."

Shoving him out of the way, Bax pushed on down the hall, his growl ringing out. "Asshole."

"Fuck you." He caught up before Bax managed to get the door open. "Come on, man. Open the fucking door."

"What, you need to piss or something? You had to go that bad you could have gone downstairs." Bax fumbled, hands stiff on the little keycard.

"What is your goddamn issue?" He grabbed the card, slammed it in the reader, the little thing bending right in half. "God *damn* it!" Jason was going to fucking kill something.

"Shit, Mini. That was the stupidest thing I've seen today." Bax grabbed his ass, then dug in Jason's jeans for his wallet, pulling out the other key.

"Well, it's the dumbest thing I've done today, so we're even." If Bax kept touching his butt, he was fixin' to be embarrassed. Embarrassing. Whichever.

"Jesus fuck." They sprang apart, Bax finally getting the door open. And damned near letting it slam in his face.

He tossed his gear into the closet and just turned right back around to head out. The edge of the motherfucking door caught him on the riding arm and he growled, punching at it and denting the living fuck out of the wood.

Son of a bitch, that hurt.

"What the fuck? Are you trying to get us charged for room damages?" Bax caught the back of his shirt and hauled his ass back into the room, flinging him in a wide circle.

He stumbled over a pair of boots, landing hard on his butt. Thank God he was used to falling, because he sprang up swinging, catching Bax square in the belly. "Fucker!"

"Oomph." Doubling over, Bax grabbed his breadbasket, cussing viciously. "You sorry son of a bitch." Andy came right after him, launching up to grapple with him, hands punching and pinching.

"Don't you—" He grunted, turning as Bax caught a nipple, tweaking it hard. "Fuck! Don't you talk about my momma like that." He grabbed a hold of Bax's belt, jerking the bastard off his nipple.

"Oh, for fuck's sake. It's a figure of— Ow! Jason!" Those eyes went wide, almost shocked, when he got a little too close to the package with his scrabbling hand.

"Sorry." He just stopped, stepped back and gave them both some room. *Fuck.* Fuck, he just needed... "I'm gonna jump in the shower." Cool down. Jack off. Scream. Something.

"Yeah. Yeah, okay. I... Go on. I'll get us both a beer." Andy wouldn't look at him, always a sign that Bax was feeling sorry as Hell.

"Okay." He didn't wait to see what Bax did—he just locked himself in the bathroom and leaned back against the door. His cock was full and aching like a sore tooth and he got one hand around it.

Fuckhead. Beautiful bastard. Grumpy asshole fucker cowboy jackass.

Jason wanted a piece of Bax so bad he could taste it.

He stroked himself good and hard, eyes closed, the calluses on his hands so fucking right. Natural. Made him need to know what Bax's hand would feel like, how those fine fucking fingers would feel, jacking him but good.

It didn't take but a minute, the adrenaline from the ride and the fight, the knowledge that Bax would be coming back soon, his favorite fantasy — they all just worked together to shove him headlong over the edge.

Oh. Oh, shit.

Oh, Goddamn.

He caught his breath, going to wash his hand off in the sink so he didn't get spunk on his clothes.

Shower.

Beer.

Movie.

Then him and Bax could stop snarling for a while.

Maybe.

Chapter Five

Bax waited until he heard the shower start before he unzipped his damned jeans and let everything breathe. All that touching and wrestling and… Shit, Jason was a fucking wet dream.

He closed his hand right around his cock, working it out of his briefs. He moaned, low and deep, leaning against the stupid little vanity thing right by the door. His back bowed, his legs went tight, and Bax went to town, stroking off hard.

When was the last time? Man, traveling with Jason made it hard to give in to the jerk off sessions he might indulge in with someone else in the room, because what roomie wanted you calling his name at two a.m.?

Shivers traveled up and down his spine, goosebumps rising even as he started to sweat. Bax pulled harder, listening to the water run and imagining Jason in there with soap and a washcloth, touching all the places Bax wanted to touch and lick and suck…

He came hard, panting, his bad knee just buckling right up on him, sending him to the floor in a heap.

Shit.

The water clicked off in the bathroom, and Bax struggled to his feet, washing his hands at the little vanity sink and cleaning up the rest, hoping it wasn't gonna smell like a cat in heat in the room. Then he grabbed the remote and a couple of beers out of the cooler, trying to look as if he'd been relaxing or some shit.

Jason walked out, wearing nothing but a towel around his hips. A pair of soft shorts were tugged out, along with a T-shirt that he had to have seen ten thousand times. "There a bottle for me?"

"You know it, man." Oh, he could go to the bathroom and clean up with the excuse that he was gonna change. "Right there. Need to use the head."

He closed the bathroom door behind him and sighed, leaning on the sink. Thank God he was all empty, or he'd be up again in a heartbeat. He heard the TV come on, heard Jason's cell phone ring. There was Momma, looking to see how they'd done.

Lord. His sweats felt scratchy, his skin too damned hot. Sighing, Bax shook it off and headed back out, knowing Momma would want to talk to him, too.

"Here he is, Momma." Jason winked at him, tossed him the cell. "You want a burger or that shrimp and pasta deal?"

"A burger, I think. Hey, Momma. How's it going?" He'd had spaghetti at Jason's momma's. That shrimp pasta wasn't gonna live up to that.

"Hey, Andy. You were looking tired today. Real tired. You feeling okay?"

"I'm just hurtin' a little, Momma." That beer could be colder. "How's the fence holdin' up?"

"Fine. Just fine. Y'all had supper yet?" She worried about them—it was cute.

"We're fixing to order now. We snuck out a little early, you know? Got to stay the whole show tomorrow." Scratching his belly and listening to it rumble, Bax wished to hell he had her cornbread to munch on.

"Well, I hope so. You both make the short go tomorrow, now. I like to see my boys' names up there."

Yeah. Yeah, she did. "We'll see. Jason will be there for sure." That man was on a roll that wouldn't quit.

"Sure. He wants you up there too, you know."

Yep, he sure did know. Jason was in his fucking corner, balls to bones. "I know. Love you, Momma. You want to talk to Mini again?" He sure wasn't in the mood to discuss why he wasn't riding so well.

"Nah, he already told me y'all were going to that

Invitational up north. I'll see you after, during the break."

"Okay. Well, you keep rooting for us. We'll see you then."

They hung up, Bax tossing the little phone back to Jason. Man, it got quiet, but for the TV.

"I got us dessert—banana splits." Well, now. There was an olive branch.

"Oh, you know I like those. They come with the strawberry stuff and the pineapple?" See him. See him stop snarling.

"Yep. Cherries and nuts, too." They shared a grin, both of them twelve again, chuckling at the hovering bad joke.

"Well, there you go. What's on CMT?" There didn't look to be any good westerns or blow 'em up movies on.

"*Dukes of Hazzard*. Again." Jason just rolled his eyes.

"Any bass fishing on?" He'd take that over some sissy reality show.

"I... Oh, dude. College rodeo." The man was obsessed. Really. Unnatura—

Shit, look at that roper go.

"We need to go to the roping pen during the break." His roping hand was terrible, but he sure did love it.

"You know it. Those cutting horses need some work, too, if we're going to round up the remuda and take 'em to Fort Worth. I think them yellow ones will throw good foals." Jason was always fucking looking for an angle.

"Sure. We can do that." Hell, he was happy enough to hitch his wagon to Jason. Mini was way smarter than him. At least that was what Jason told him every day.

That had him grinning, the last of his mean bone dying down.

The food came then, and they got themselves well and truly settled—burgers and fries and salad and ice cream and beer. Oh. Better.

Bax kicked back, patting his belly. "I tell you what, it's amazing what a little food will do."

"You know it." Jason leaned against the pillows, rolling his feet in circles.

"You stiff?" Okay, that sounded nasty, but he wouldn't

say no if Mini needed a massage.

"Just a little." Jason grabbed one ankle, pulling and stretching.

Bax watched every move, his hands clenching and unclenching. "Want some help?"

"Sure."

Now that was a special type of torture. The whole wanting to touch, getting to touch, but not in the way he wanted... Well. Yeah. He moved on over to Jason's bed, letting his hands land on that one ankle, just resting there a moment to warm it up before he started work.

Man, that left ankle was tense, just a little swollen. Jason was going to have to watch that. "You need to wrap, Mini. 'Fore you tear something."

"You think so? I hate the way that feels in the boot."

"I know that." He surely did get tired of hearing the bitching. But that was better than snapping something and missing the finals.

Jason rumbled a little, sat up. "Did I piss in your Wheaties somehow, man? You've been hunting my ass since we left the arena."

"Huh?" His head snapped up, his eyes meeting Jason's. "No. I mean... I'm just punchy, okay? And you're in range."

"Okay." Mini seemed to get that okay, nodded at him once. "I'll wrap it."

"Good. You're doing too good this year, man." He dug his thumbs into the muscles of Jason's calf, the shorts giving him plenty of access.

"Uhn." Jesus, that sound was sex. Pure, raw sex. "I want it bad, Bax. I can fucking taste it."

"I want it too, man. You have no idea." Such a dangerous thing, touching Jason like that. Bax kept on, though, all the way up to that knee.

"I do. I know." Jason arched a little, toes curling. "That's... Didn't know I was so tense..."

"Mmmhmm. You were really tight. Hard." Oh, yeah. He was working on hard as if he hadn't come an hour ago.

29

Jason's eyes were closed, cheeks flushed as he nodded. "Needed a good rub-down, huh?"

"Uh-huh." His voice sounded like frogs had gotten stuck in his throat. "Sometimes a man does."

"You know it, Bax." He wasn't the only one tenting—that T-shirt couldn't hide Jason's happy.

All he had to do was reach out and touch... Higher... He wanted to. Oh, God, he wanted to. If they'd both had three or four more beers, he might. Instead he just sat there with his teeth in his mouth, hands on Jason's skin, staring.

Those too-pretty-to-be-a-guy's eyes popped open, looking right at him, just not backing off a bit. *Jesus. Jesus fuck.*

The banging on the door had him jumping up off the bed like he'd been shot.

"Andy! Jase! Bunch of us are going out to shoot pool. Wanna?"

Well, that had taken his cock right down. Clearing his throat, he headed for the door, cracking it open. "Depends on who's buying."

AJ grinned, that front tooth missing. Man, Missy was going to kill him. "Shit, man. Jase won the round. He's buying!"

"Sure. You just ask him if he wants to. He's changed and all." Everyone knew Mini was in for the night if he was wearing those fuzzy shorts.

"Oh, dude. He's already out of the jeans?" AJ sighed, shook his head. "We meeting for breakfast?"

"Yeah. We'll do the buffet." They got discounts and shit. They might as well take advantage of it.

"Cool. Night, y'all." As he shut the door, he could hear AJ. "Jase was already in the bed, y'all. He ain't coming."

"What am I? Chopped liver?" Bax winked at Jason, wandering back to his own bed and staring at the TV.

"Nah, they all just know us, huh?" Jason looked over, winked back. "Antisocial assholes that we are."

"Yeah. Well. Did I mention I'm old?" He'd been a lot more social, once upon a time. But that was for the kids.

"Once or twice. We got a couple more go-rounds in us, man. No giving up on me."

"Not about to." No, sir. That man was gonna be a champion. Even if he couldn't ride the circuit anymore, he'd be there for Jason.

Even if it killed him.

Chapter Six

"Man, look at Andy! He's gonna get him some!" AJ handed Jason a beer, Buck coming to stand on the other side of him.

"Yeah, it's about time." Bastard, out there dancing with that little blonde gal like he hadn't blown the hell out of his knee in the short go. Amazing what a fucking cortisone shot would do for a man who came in third for the event.

That part was okay — the third part. Bax needed a couple of rides.

But the blonde part? The dancing part on that knee?

Not so much.

Asshole.

Bax had a goofy smile frozen on his face, swinging that gal around to the Fireman like she was a ball on a rope. Jesus, that knee was gonna be three times its normal size. Hell, Jason's heart had about stopped when Bax had gotten hung up on the dismount, doing a full-on helicopter to the ground. He'd seen Bax's face go pale as milk and he'd just barely kept himself from doing more than meeting the stubborn bastard at the gate.

Now that damned fool was chugging Jack and Coke and acting like he was a fifteen year old at his first barn dance.

The song ended and Bax gave the little buckle bunny a kiss on the cheek, walking her back to her giggling friends before huffing and puffing back to Jason.

"Hey." He scooted over, gave Bax a place to prop. The boys were hooting and slapping Bax's back, giving him shit.

Bax grinned, but the man wasn't blushing a bit, so Jason relaxed. That meant it was just a little blowing off steam.

He sucked back his beer, the liquid break hitting his empty belly hard. "You want another, man? I need a beer."

Or four.

"Yeah. I'd better switch to beer, though." Yeah, Bax was more than a little blinky.

"'Kay." Jason headed over to the line, only having to talk to thirty people on the way.

Jesus.

Ten bucks for two beers and he still had to wait half an hour for it.

Bax had found them a sitting table by the time he got back, and that leg was propped up on another chair. Yeah, and Bax's mouth was set in a hard line.

The boys had deserted him, AJ on the dance floor, Buck with an arm around some buckle bunny. He handed the beer over, nodded. "There's pills up in the room, if you need it."

"I'll think on it." Winking, Bax toasted him with the beer. "I been hittin' the sauce a bit too much for the good pills."

"Yeah. Least for a couple hours. You were sure shaking a leg, man." He slugged some back, the cold brew just what he needed.

"Well, you know I have to once in a while." Now Bax was ducking his head, not quite meeting Jason's eyes.

"Yep. Good ride today, huh?" Fuck, this was weird.

And dark.

And loud.

"Yeah. Yeah, for both of us. You rocked it out on Booger." That had Bax looking at him again, that deep pleasure Bax took in his riding right there.

"Yeah. It felt good. Damn good." He gave Bax a grin, a nod. Hell, Momma'd called them both, just squealing.

"Nothing wrong with first and third at all, Mini." They knocked fists together, laughing like fools.

"No, sir. Nothing wrong with that at all." Hell, no. They couldn't hardly ask for more.

They sat a bit, Bax turning down a couple of pretty,

sparkly girls who sidled up to ask him to dance. By the time the third girl had wandered off, Jason was noticing at the lines carved out around Bax's mouth.

"It's time to go up, buddy. Take one of them pills." He knew that look, knew it bone deep.

"Yeah. Yeah, I think it is. I've been off the booze long enough now, huh?" Hell, Bax could outdrink most of the young kids, still.

"Yeah. Come on. Let's go." They'd walk out then he could help some when they got away from the damn crowd.

Bax stood up real careful like, but seeming pretty damned normal. Only Jason knew what it cost, because he could see those hands he loved so much clench almost white. They got out of the crush and in an empty hallway before he scooted up, gave Bax a shoulder to lean on. "Come on. We're right by the elevator."

"'Kay." Man, Bax was panting by now, stumbling a little. Good thing they didn't have to chance the escalator.

"I got you." *Shit. Shit, don't let it be something worse than... Well, don't let it be something real bad.*

"Stop your mother-henning, Mini. I just twisted it up, is all. God knows I been hurt enough to know." That would have been way more convincing if Bax wasn't leaning on him so hard.

"Yeah, yeah. You know me, all sensitive and shit." He propped Bax up, hit the button for the nineteenth floor.

Chuckling, Bax nodded. "Yep. You're some kind of sweetheart..." They slipped in before someone else joined them, heading right on up to the room.

"That's me. Sweetness and fucking light. Pure joy to be around." They both got to snorting, leaning into each other with it.

They managed to finagle Bax into the room, and Jason eased him down on the bed, making sure not to jostle. Bax groaned, leaning back on his elbows, eyes closed. He grabbed two of the good pills, handed them over along with the fucking remote then started working on getting

34

Bax's boots off.

"Thanks, man. Oh. Oh, easy." Shit, that leg went like stone, hard as hell under those jeans. Bax was hurtin' some.

He straddled Bax's calf, squeezing it good and firm between his legs so he could pull without jostling that knee too bad.

"Jesus!" The sound exploded right out of Bax, but the boot popped off finally, leaving him with a gnarly damned sock.

"Sorry, man. Had to be done." He wet a couple of rags, tossed one in the ice bucket with the melted ice and the other in the little microwave. "Get yer jeans off."

"Okay." Wiggling, Bax shimmied out of the jeans, grunting a little as the tight denim tried to slide past the swollen knee. "Man, I did it up right."

"Yup. Hot first, then cold." They both knew the drill and Jason brought over one of the big bath towels to prop Bax up on.

"You could go back and party with the guys if you wanted," Bax said, rolling the towel up and putting it gingerly under his leg. "You don't have to take care of me, Mini."

"Shut up." Jason grabbed the hot washrag, bouncing it back and forth between his hands before dropping it on that swolled up knee.

"Oh. Fuck a duck." The heat worked, though. It surely did. He could see all of Bax's muscles start to uncurl.

Jason gave it five minutes before switching to the cold and getting the rag heated up again. Bax winced at the icy-cold one.

"Weenie. Shit, that's just water. I need to go refill the bucket."

"Okay. I... Thanks, Jase. Sorry." Okay, what was Bax's deal now? Moody bastard.

"Sorry for what?" He whapped Bax's shoulder. "Stop it, man. I'll grab a couple Cokes, some ice. We'll play cards for a few hours."

Just like always.

"Sounds good, man. I'm just a little blinky." Poor Bax sounded on the stupid side of slow, not quite drunk, but better than tipsy.

"Yeah. Yeah. You just sit a minute. I'll get you set up right and tight." That was what a friend was good for.

"Okay. Can we have ice cream?" Lord, that man was an addict. Really, really.

"Shit, yeah. Call down to room service. Tell 'em to bring that and coffee."

"Gotcha." Fumbling, Bax grabbed the phone and punched in room service. Jason almost bust a gut trying not to laugh at the man's rambling order, and the fact that suddenly they were getting onion rings and cheesecake and some fruit thing, too.

Still, onion rings sounded damned good. Jason waited until Bax gave their room number before heading to get ice. Not that he didn't trust Mister Stoned, but they didn't need him ordering a fucking rack of lamb or some shit.

When he got back, Bax was sprawled out on the bed, arms and legs flung wide, naked as a jaybird. The only thing he had on was the wet washcloth.

Lord, lord. "Man, did your clothes explode while I was down the hall?"

"Huh?" One dark brown eye peered at him, cracking open with effort. "No... Got hot. Like burny."

"You gotta have some water, man." Jason moved the cold rag up to Bax's chest, hot rag back on the knee. See him. See him not looking at Andy's privates.

Not.

Not not not.

"You think? Fuck, I hate those pills." They worked, though. Bax's color was better, even if he was sweating like a lathered bronc.

"Yeah, I know. Let me get another rag cooled off. You can wipe down." Wipe down. Cool off. Put some fucking shorts on before he embarrassed himself.

"'Kay." Sitting up, Bax glanced around, blinking. "We're

in a hotel."

"Yep. Not a bad one, either. Have something to drink." He opened the top of the Coke, started wiping Bax's shoulders.

"Thanks." That tanned throat worked as Bax swallowed, giving Jason more to gawk at. Thank God, really, because he didn't need to be sneaking any more peeks at Bax's dangly parts. Which were nice.

"Anytime."

Nice and looking as if they needed someone to touch them.

Lick them.

Yeah.

Nice.

"You okay?" Bax's eyes popped open, staring right into his, one hand coming up to steady him when he all but fell over.

"Uh-huh." He was fixin' to just...blow.

"Okay. Did you know that the bed is all spinny, Jase? Feels like I'm back on Lawnmower."

Oh, that would be funny if Jason hadn't been so horny. "Yeah, man. But you're not hurting, huh?" He could just... back off. "Let me get a cold rag."

"No! Mini, I swear. I'm going to fly right off the bed." Andy's hand tightened on his shoulder as if he was the one solid thing in Bax's world.

"I ain't gonna let you fall, buddy." He eased Bax back, one knee resting beside that lean hip.

"Oh. Okay." Hand sliding to rest on his leg, Bax laid back and let him do some pampering, smiling like a fool at him.

His cock beat against his zipper, hands running that damn rag over Bax's chest.

Look at those little nipples...

"No sense in looking at me that way, Mini. Someone will just knock on the door. It's like, the universe is against us." Okay, now Bax was babbling.

"Yeah. Yeah, room service. With your fucking ice cream." It actually made it easier—he didn't want to take advantage of Bax when the bastard was stoned.

He wanted to take advantage when Bax knew which end was, uh, up.

"Sure would be nice, though. To not have to go jack off in the shower." Patting him, Bax kinda wandered, switching off to talk about Momma and how she needed to marry Jack.

Lord, lord. He chuckled, nodded, listening to that stupid son of a bitch go on. One of these days, man. They'd both be fucked up at the same time again and get a little something.

The ice cream and shit came, and that seemed to perk Bax up, getting some food in his stomach. Perked him up enough that Bax finally looked down at himself and blushed, grabbing some sweats.

Jason didn't bother saying nothing. There wasn't nothing to say.

Not yet.

Chapter Seven

The crowd was pumped. Clapping, screaming, ready to rumble.

The mood behind the chutes was about as jumped up. The guys were like a bunch of long-tailed cats in a room full of rocking chairs, everyone knowing that the best bulls in the business were right there tonight.

Bax sat on the rail, watching Jason warm up. He'd done his own calisthenics already, as he was two rides ahead of Jase on the order. That was good, though. He'd get to pull the man's rope. Watching Jason rough up his glove was like watching a porno tape of a man jacking off.

They'd done the intro, the singing and the praying, and now all that was left was the riding. Bax had drawn Hamburger, which he wasn't thrilled about. That damned bull would pull you down and try to put your eye out.

Jason bent and rolled, shoulders working, tight little ass shifting. "You feeling it, cowboy?"

"Yeah. Yeah, I am. Gonna be a Hell of a night." It was always really good or really bad when that kind of energy was pumping through an arena. "You ready? You pulled Ghostrider."

"You know it. He's a good 'un." Hell, yes. Jason'd ridden that big old beast for 86.25 points last year, sweet as honey.

"Well, you keep your mind in the middle." The announcer called up AJ, and he and Jason both leaned over the fence, shouting Aje on.

Round and round...six, seven...

"Yes!" They both started hooting and clapping, Jason slapping his shoulder. "Look at that! AJ! You might feed

39

them babies!"

Bax pumped a fist in the air, cheering hard himself. "I told you, didn't I? He's a good 'un. And he needed the ride."

"No shit." AJ hopped up, trailing his bull rope and grinning ear-to-ear.

"Look at you, man. You almost acted like a bull rider." Jason chuckled, winked at AJ.

"Way to go, man." He clapped AJ on the back. "Now, someone come on and pull my damned rope." Bax was up in two more rides.

"Bitch, bitch, bitch." Jason was right there with him, hand on his shoulder. "Keep your fucking head up on this one."

Like he didn't know that.

"Chin down, chest out, blah blah." He'd been on his first fucking calf before Mini was even born. *Asshole.* He climbed over the rail, balancing on his hands while he dropped his knees and let the bull know he was there.

"Smart-ass. You break your jaw, you'll be sucking chicken from a straw." Jason's hands were in his vest.

Good thing, too, because that big bastard reared up and yanked down, trying to bash his brains in on the rail. *Fuck.* Bax clenched his jaw, getting set, his rope good and tight in his riding hand.

Then he gave the nod.

He got one good leap, then that little bastard started spinning, solid as a top.

Hot damn. The G-forces yanked at him, pulling his riding arm almost out of the damned socket, but his free arm stayed nice and up, his outside leg spurred without him even trying, and when the fucking buzzer sounded he was still on top.

Goddamn.

The fucking crowd went wild, Nate waving his arms as Bax fought to let loose of his rope.

His hand just didn't want to let go, Goddamn it, and just about the time he thought he'd ride another eight seconds, his legs flipped over and he went down into the well, hanging off the side like a tick on a dog.

Fuck. Fuck, he ran like a moonshiner with a posse after him. He could hear Jeff and Nate hollering, feel somebody's hands tugging the living shit out of him. His hand finally popped free, his chest bouncing off the bull's ribs, sending him reeling.

He heard bellering, heard the bull's hooves hitting the dirt, but what he heard above all that was Jason's voice. "Goddamn it, Baxter! Move your slow ass!"

Scrambling, he crawled as fast as he could, Coke finally grabbing his vest and hauling him off toward the chutes. Jesus.

Jason and AJ yanked him up, holding him against the fence. "You good? Bax? Talk to me, man. You rode that mean bastard!"

"Huh?" Shaking it off, he tested all his muscles, trying to see if everything worked. "Yeah, yeah, it's good."

"You fucking know it! Eighty nine point five, cowboy. Go tip your hat to your fans!"

Bax jumped off the fence and stepped back out into the arena and threw his hat, pumping his arms to get the crowd screaming for him.

Hot damn.

The fans went fucking crazy, Cooper Riley bouncing over with his hat, Coke slapping his ass. Goddamn. That was it. Just fucking like that, top of the leader board for now and almost surely in the money.

He climbed back up the fence instead of going through the gate. He'd be pulling rope for Mini soon.

The chutes were buzzing, the guys giving him shit, teasing and laughing with him. Jason was nodding, the bastard waiting for him with a shit-eating grin.

"You see that, Mini?" He knew Jason had, because the fine son of a bitch had been right there when he'd almost gotten his ass stomped, but now everything wasn't a blur. He could see that fucking million dollar smile.

"You know it. You owned that fucker."

He had. He hadn't had a ride like that in months. "Felt good, Jase. Felt amazing. You have to do better. You ought to be the one to win the go-round." His season was never gonna be as good as Jason's. He wasn't stupid enough to think it, either.

"Shut up and bask, Bax." Jason winked, pulled his glove out. "Come on. Let's get this one down."

"You got it." Grinning, he sort of wallowed in his almost ninety point ride. Goddamn, it felt good. He stepped over the rails to the stand on the outside of the gate, ready to pull.

Jason hopped over, all business, eyes on the prize. It took some nudging and pushing—that bull was wanting to crouch, not happy at all about this whole working deal. Spoiled thing. AJ wedged a boot in between the bull and the fence, and Kyle got the four by four out, and soon enough they got Mini settled, that loose old bull rope settled in place. Man rode on the fucking end of his fingers.

He got a look, serious as all get out. "Let's do it."

Then, as soon as he was out of the way, Mini nodded, the gate swinging open.

The bull turned right out away from Jason's hand, which was always a tough ride, the force pulling down and across. Jason had better balance than anyone Bax had ever seen, though. He could do it. The seconds stretched out. One... two...three...

He could fucking see it, when the ride went south, the bull jerking back into Jason's hand, the tug pulling that bull rope almost out of Jason's grip, Jason heading right over to the side of the bull. Six... Seven...

Shit. Shit, Mini was gonna make the ride, but there was no way there was gonna be a good get off. Bax started yelling at about eight and a half seconds, when Jason's legs both flipped to the same side of the bull.

"Mini! Goddamn it, Jason! Get out of there!"

About that time, Jason spun, feet blown right out from under him, head connecting with horn with a thwack the

42

whole arena could hear almost as well as the thud as Jason hit the ground, right under those hooves.

Bax was off the fence and in the arena before he even thought about it. Coke was shouting the bull's name, bouncing like a jack in the box, but he saw the bull moving away out of the corner of his eye. He slid to his knees next to Jason, reaching for the man, babbling something like a prayer.

There wasn't anything in those open eyes — not a fucking thing, which was the creepiest thing on Earth up till the second Jason when stiff as a board, legs thrumming on the dirt.

Oh. Oh, no. Oh, fuck no.

All he could do was kneel at Jason's head and try to hold that convulsing body as still as he could. The sports medicine guys got there just as Jason's hands started clenching and unclenching, the weirdest sound coming from him.

"Get me the backboard. Jason? Jason, you know where you are, son?"

The guys were all around, hiding Mini from the crowd, from the cameras, as best they could.

"Jason!" Bax barked it out, knowing Jason would never respond to all that gentle coaxing. "Damn it, Mini. Talk to me."

One hand came up, Doc grabbing it. "Keep talking."

Those eyes just kept rolling.

Fuck, he felt sick. His belly just heaved, but Bax wasn't gonna stop to think about his own shit. "Jason. Come on, buddy. You want to hear your score, right? You need to come on and say something so I know you're not all broke, you asshole."

"Out." He could just hear the word, forced past that clenched jaw and he could just hoot with it.

Yes. Yes, that's right, you stubborn motherfucker. Don't let yourself get embarrassed out here on the floor.

"We got to get him up, get him out of here." If Jason could move and talk then he could get upright enough to get dragged out. And not on the backboard. "We're gonna lift you now, Jason. I swear to God, you don't stay straight, I'll let AJ drive your truck."

"Out."

They got him moving, the silent crowd going wild all around them. AJ had one arm and he had the other, his shoulder pushed up into Jason's armpit, holding the man up.

Those legs were moving, Jason trying to walk, and Bax tried hard not to sag with relief. That probably meant Mini's back was okay. Or at least not broken up in pieces. Not that he still wasn't worried, but Bax figured Jason could out-stubborn anything that wasn't spinal.

They made it to sports medicine, got Mini laid out on a bed. Doc Madding nodded toward the door, lips in a tight line. "Y'all get."

"Not leaving." No way. Bax stared the Doc down, then nodded at AJ. "Keep everyone out."

"You got it."

AJ was a good 'un. He'd do what they asked.

Doc was in Jason's face, shaking his shoulder a little, trying to get the son of a bitch to wake up right.

"Out. Out. Out!" Now *that* was fucked.

"Okay. Get the EMTs in here. He needs a CAT scan. Now." Doc Madding never snapped at his staff like that.

The doc was snarling, turning to get his assistant to move faster, and Bax leaned down quick like, trying to get Jason to focus on him. "Mini? Come on, Mini. Say my name."

Jason's eyes rolled like dice, moving faster, as if Mini was dreaming, was looking for him. "B—"

"That's it." He grabbed the one hand that kept flailing. "Don't do this to me, Jason. Don't you get all messed up on me now."

"Ba..."

"We need to move him, Andy. Get out of the way, now. He's got to go." Doc moved between them, just like that.

"Doc. I... He needs me." He met the doc's worried eyes,

44

trying to get the man to understand. "Let me go with him." He'd throw a fit like no one would believe, the doc made him stay behind.

Doc stared at him a long second, gray eyes moving back and forth, and he could feel that fit building when Doc nodded. "Go get his stuff, meet me in two minutes in the loading dock."

Yeah, they'd need Jason's information and he'd have to call Momma. The wreck'd be on the TV in an hour. He got his ass in gear, heading out, nodding at AJ again. "I'm going with him. You just tell them all he'll be fine."

He went to get Jason's gear and his own, keeping his eyes down so he didn't have to answer questions.

Goddamn it, Jason would have to be fine.

Anything else just wasn't gonna fly.

Chapter Eight

There was something beeping, steady and irritating as all fuck.

Beep. Beep. Beep. Beep.

Jesus fucking Christ.

"Bax, turn that fucking alarm off before I kill you."

Shit, his throat hurt like a motherfucker and this was the darkest hotel room on earth. What had he fucking been drinking last night?

"Mini? Oh, Jesus, fuck. You in there finally?"

What the hell did that mean?

"I di'n stay out all night, did I?" He tried to sit up, stopping short when all sorts of things starting screaming, mainly his fucking head.

"You got stomped, Jase." Bax's hands were good and familiar on him, easing him back down to the bed, couch, whatever. "Took a bad one to the head."

"Huh?" Oh, that was better. Easier. "I feel like shit." Thank God the fucking lights were down—he might hurl.

"Yeah. I swear, Mini. You've been out solid." Bax was just petting his chest, fingers moving slow and easy. Soothing.

"This...this ain't sports medicine..." Sports medicine wasn't dark like this, not ever, not in any arena, and he couldn't hear the crowd.

"No." That hard edged voice went all hushed. "You're in the hospital, Jase."

"Whut?" He shook his head, blinking fast, his belly churning. "No. No, man. Turn the fucking lights on. This ain't right."

It wasn't right at all. They were fucking with him.

Somebody was fucking with him. There wasn't a fucking hospital on earth like this.

"The lights? Mini, they're turned down in here, but they're on. I swear, I was wondering how you could sleep." That hand flattened on his chest, pressing a little, holding him in place.

"Goddamn it, Andy Baxter! You quit fucking with me! You stop it right fucking now!" This wasn't funny. Not even a little. He shoved as hard as he could, hands connecting with Bax's arm, the slap loud and sharp.

"Jase! Quit it! You'll hurt yourself. They said you got to stay still." Bax sounded panicked, but he sure couldn't see it for shit. It was too damned dark. "Listen, I'll turn the overhead on, okay? Okay? Just hold on."

He heard the click. Heard it.

No.

No fucking way.

No. Fucking. Way.

He ground his teeth together, hands going up to rub his eyes, touch them. They were there, dry and a little scratchy. He rubbed harder.

Come on. Come on now.

"Jase?" Bax was back, fingers wrapping around his wrists. "What? What is it? Do you need the Doc?"

"I. I. I gotta get up. I gotta wash my face." He could fucking feel Bax, right there, and he looked, looked as hard as he could and there wasn't nothing.

Nothing.

Jesus fucking Christ.

"No. No, you need to stay down. Your brain got all shook around in your skull. I'll get a cloth." He could hear Bax get up, boots clicking on the linoleum floor, could hear the water run.

Oh, fuck. Fuck. Okay. Okay. Okay.

He squeezed his eyes shut tight, trying to figure what day it was, what had happened. He remembered driving from the Marriott over to the arena. Remembered the fucking sun being so hot there in Phoenix that it burned his hands on the steering wheel. "We're in Phoenix."

"Yeah. Yeah. Good." The cloth felt wet and cool on his forehead, his cheeks. "That's good, Mini."

"Bax." He took the rag, started scrubbing his eyes good and hard, wanting to get something. Anything.

"What? What is it? What hurts?" Again, Bax grabbed his wrists, stopping him. "You got to quit that, honey."

"I can't." He could hear his heart, hear it pounding in his head as if someone was beating him with a stick — *bang bang bang*. "I cain't! Let me go! I got to get out of here. Bax, you get me out of here, right fucking now!"

Yanking him upright, Bax wrapped wiry arms around him, keeping him still. "I can't, Mini. I... You got to have tests and shit. Please. Please, just calm the fuck down and tell me what's wrong!"

"I cain't see. I cain't see nothing." He grabbed a hold of Bax, fingers fisting in the man's shirt. "I cain't see, Andy."

Bax went absolutely still, his breath even hitching to a halt. "What? They said you didn't hurt your eyes at all."

"It's nothing but dark. Not nothing. You gotta get me out of here, Bax." He couldn't be here.

"Okay." One hand slid up and down his back, stroking, warming him where the chills had come up. "Okay. I'll get you out. But you have to agree to see a private doctor."

"You take me home. You take me home, Goddamn it."

The door opened, footsteps sounding. "Mr. Scott, you're awake. How're you feeling?"

"He's just fine, Doc. But he has to pee. Can we give him a minute in the head?" Bax sounded so reasonable. So fucking calm. But the grip on his arm was anything but.

"Are you sure you're up to walking around? You've got some serious swelling in the back of your brain, son. That can mess with your perception for a few days, give you blind spots. It shouldn't last."

Oh. Oh, thank God. Thank God. "I'll be careful. I'm good. I know where I am and shit. I just gotta do my business."

It shouldn't last.

Okay.

Okay, cool.

"I'll give him a hand, Doc. He's the stubbornest cuss on earth." Bax stood him up, all careful like, hand under his arm. Then Bax took him to the bathroom, helping him figure out where stuff was. "You gotta be cool, Mini," Bax whispered. "Or they won't let you go home."

"Yeah. Yeah, okay. You heard him. It shouldn't last." He got his face wet, hands shaking—he could feel them.

"Exactly. I told you, you're all swole. But if you let him know you're all hinky he'll keep you here."

Yeah. Yeah, okay—he'd faked it before.

"You...you do good in the round?" Hell, he didn't remember if the event was over, nothing after driving to the arena.

"I did. I got eighty nine and some. Went to the short go yesterday on it. Didn't ride for shit."

The soft, wry laughter had him grinning despite himself.

"Everybody else move on? You called Momma?"

"I did. She wanted to come but I told her to make shit right at home for you. AJ went on, but he said we could go to his ranch if we needed."

"I just want to go home. I— Wait. Where was Bax going next? How the hell was he supposed to...?

Fuck. Fuck. Shit.

"I got a bye for the next event. We'll figure it from there." Hell, the man always could read his mind.

"Yeah? I'm sorry, Bax. I just... I can't figure this yet." He wanted to just scream.

"No. No, it's cool, Jase." Those hands turned him, pushing him and pulling, helping him do his business. Which he still could do. Jesus.

"Okay." He got himself together, grinding his teeth, staying right there with Bax. "What next? Did the doctor go?"

"No. He's gonna wanna talk to you." Those lips pressed

almost to his ear. "I'll walk you through it."

Bax was solid as a rock. Always right there.

"Okay. Okay, Bax." Jason set his jaw, nodded.

Okay, open the fucking gate.

Chapter Nine

Rolling his shoulders, Bax hunted for the next turnoff, knowing that it was coming up soon and that he was tired enough to miss it. They had half an hour to Momma's, and Jason was sleeping, wore out from being all scrambled like an egg by that monster bull.

The fact that Jason still couldn't see had his gut feeling like one of them fancy knots he'd read about in high school. Something Greek, maybe. Hopefully once the damned fool settled in and rested a bit, the swelling would go down and everything would go back to right.

If anyone could make Jason take it easy, it would be Momma.

They started to pass a truck stop, and Bax made the decision to pull in almost too late, whipping them hard enough to wake Jason up. It wasn't any easier this time than it had been any other time in the last sixteen fucking hours, either.

Jason flailed, looking around, trying so fucking hard to see. "Bax? Bax?"

"Right here, Mini. You're in the car. I need a drink and a piss. You sit and wake up a minute, we'll go in." He just couldn't leave Jase in the car. Not now, not any time in the last three days.

"I... Okay. Okay. Where are we?" Jason looked like hammered shit, bruises popping up like fucking daisies. It was fucking weird, because Jason would stare at him sometimes.

They'd found them a city doctor that didn't know dick about them or where they'd come from. That dude

51

had explained that the whole sight thing was because of pressure or some shit, so Jason's eyes would track, but it still freaked him out. "We're not far from Momma's. I just needed to stop and stretch."

"Okay. You can go in. I'll just sit here." Jason pulled the brim of his hat down farther, hiding his face.

"Nope. I ain't leaving you alone out here. Come on, Mini. Cowboy up." He got out and went around to open Jason's door.

It was getting harder for Jason to follow, that jaw set stubborn against moving, even as the son of a bitch slid from the truck. "I fucking hate this."

"I know." Hell, yes, he knew. He could see it in every line of that lean body. He took Jason's hand and put it on his arm, just a little. Just to guide him. "Nice and easy."

The door opened, a bunch of teenagers tumbling out, laughing and goofing off. Jason stopped short, shook his head. "Just let me go back to the truck. What if —?"

"What if nothing. You ain't no pussy. Now get your ass in gear and come on. I got to pee." Tough love was better than nothing, right? He couldn't let Jason lose what he was.

Jason ducked his head, growling low and following him. Those fingers were shaking, digging into his arm and Goddamn, it broke his heart.

He bit it back, though, because Jason wouldn't want it. Not that kind of sympathy. Jason needed him to just know what to do. Even if he didn't.

They hit the head, and he got Jason set up before doing his own thing. Then they washed up and went for drinks.

"You want a root beer?"

"Yeah, if they got Barq's. If not, I'll take a Dr. Pepper."

"Cool." Picky bastard. He grabbed them both a drink and some of those weird maple peanuts Jason loved. He found himself some beef jerky, too. Jason didn't say anything, kept his head down and stuck right there. Baxter could feel his fucking heart beating against one arm. Biting his lip, Bax took them to the register to pay, keeping his face under his hat. This was local enough to be dangerous.

"Y'all look like you been through a hell of a fight, guys." The little gum-popping girl didn't seem to recognize them, but Jason still stiffened.

"You should see the other guys," Bax said, winking at her from under his hat brim and handing over a twenty. "Thanks, honey. Come on, buddy. Time to hit the road."

Jason nodded. "'Night."

The little gal beamed, nodded, and off they went. Christ.

Sighing his relief, Bax settled Jason in the truck again, eyeing the driver's side with a baleful stare. His shoulder was gonna fall right off. His cell started going off and he didn't even have to look to see it was Momma. Lord have mercy. The woman had radar.

"'Lo?" He slid into the truck, turning to mouth "*Momma*" to Jason before he realized Mini wouldn't see it.

"Where are y'all? How's Jason? How're you? I got y'all both appointments with Dr. Dewey in the morning tomorrow and I got coffee brewing and beds made..."

Jesus Christ on a crutch.

He eased the truck out, making sure those teenagers were well out of the way. "We're not far, Momma. Jason's resting. We'll be there soon."

"Has it got better? His eyes? There's been reporters calling and the folks from the tour, too, wanting to know what's up. I didn't tell them nothing. You know I don't hold with that."

"I know." Thank God for that. "Nothin's changed, 'cept he's gotten meaner." Bax jumped when Jason pinched his thigh. "We'll be home in a jiffy, Momma. I got to drive."

"Okay, honey. You be careful and y'all come let me take care of my boys. I know you're tired, Andy."

"Yes, ma'am." He was. It was starting to set in, the worst of the sore. It always came a couple of days after the crash. "Bye."

They hung up, and he whapped Jason on the arm. "No pinching."

Jason reached out, pinched him again. "Stop me, then."

His hand clamped down on Jason's wrist. "Goddamn it, Mini. Quit it."

Jason jerked away, the momentum sending one hand smashing into the dash, the crack even sounding like it hurt.

"Shit. Shit. I'm sorry." He was just edgy as a cat on a tin roof. The truck jerked a little, his bad arm not able to hold her steady. "You okay?"

"Yeah." Jason sat there for a minute or two, blinking real slow, looking green as hell. "Stop the truck, Bax."

"'Kay." He slammed to the shoulder, threw open his door, and ran around to help Jason out.

Jason managed on his own though, stumbling along the shoulder until he hit the guard rail and went down, shoulders shuddering.

All Bax could do was stand there, hands hanging at his side, and make sure no one hit the truck or them. Goddamn it. God damn it.

It ended as suddenly as it started, Jason getting to his feet, that fucking jaw set again. "Sorry. I'm good."

Right.

Good.

Blind. Bruised. Swaying on his feet and pale as milk.

Right as fucking rain.

"No problem, Jase. Come on, that root beer will hit the spot, and we'll be home soon." Please God, let it be sooner than he thought. He wasn't sure how many more miles they could go.

"Yeah." Jason took a step, one hand held out. "Help me out, man."

He closed his hand around Jason's immediately, and he tugged the man back to the truck, leading him right up to fold into the cab. "You set?"

"Yeah. Yeah, Bax. I'm good."

No. Nothing was okay. Jason was just shaking, so tired and sick that he looked as if he'd been on a three day caffeine binge. Bax didn't say nothin', though. Just got in the truck and drove, his neck and back feeling like poured concrete.

When the lights of Momma's house came into view he wanted to hoot and holler. Bax settled for a, "We're here, Mini."

"Thank God."

Momma was right there, coming down the porch steps, looking like she hadn't slept in as long as he had. "Praise Jesus, my boys are home. Come on, both of you. You're home."

Jason's door was opened, and Momma pulled his skinny body out into her arms as she held on tight. Jason seemed a little panicked, really.

"Momma." Going around, he gently pulled Jase out of her arms. "Jason's hurtin' and queasy. Let's get him in and I'll get the gear. Okay?"

"Jack'll get it. He was here keeping me company."

Jack Owen nodded to him, the old cowboy headed for the truck. Jason's momma'd been taking up with old Jack for ten years and nobody so much as hinted about the fact that the man had a toothbrush in her bathroom or a coffee cup in the cabinet.

"Thanks, Jack." He cupped Jason's elbow, the bony bit fitting just right in his palm, and Bax led Mini inside, knowing those feet knew the steps even without Jase being able to see them. "Couch, honey?"

"Yeah." Those eyes were moving wildly, trying so fucking hard to see.

"You're gonna make yourself sick again." His jaw clenched, and Bax just wanted to tear something up. Goddamn it, why hadn't he been the one to get stomped? He was a washed-up old bastard. Jason was on the fucking rise. "Here you go. I'll get your drink."

He turned and Momma was standing there and staring, hand over her mouth, tears pouring down her cheeks. They all were just frozen up a second when Jack came in, nudged Momma's arm. "Brenda, lady. Go pour them boys a drink. They look tired."

Momma nodded and when she spoke, she sounded almost normal. "That they do. Coffee or Coke, boys?"

"I'll take coffee, Momma. I grabbed Jason a root beer. Doc said he needed to lay off the caffeine." His whole body throbbed, and his knees started to feel tottery, but he managed to get Jason sat down, and head over to give Momma a brusque hug.

"You done good, son. Real good." She kissed his temple. "Doctor give you anything for your sore, Andy? I got the good Tylenol."

"I'm fine, Momma." His voice cracked, and Bax just couldn't take it no more. He headed outside, tearing open the pack of smokes he'd snuck in at the truck stop.

It wasn't a minute before Jack was out there, cigarette in his teeth. "You mind?"

"Nope. Come on." Hell, maybe Jack would give him a light. "She been a bear?"

"You know it." The lighter came out, both cigarettes lit up. "How's he holding up?"

"He's hurt bad, Jack. I mean, he's moving fine, and his bruises will heal, but I'm worried as Hell about his head."

"Brenda says he cain't see?"

"Not right now. Doc says it ought to get better, but it... I dunno." His fingers clenched so hard that his cigarette broke, and Bax stubbed it out with his boot. "I just don't know."

"We'll figure it." That gravelly old voice was solid as shit, reminding him that he wasn't alone and neither was Mini. Not at all.

"We will. Thanks for coming, old man. We ought to go save Jase from his momma, yeah?" He clapped Jack on the back, wincing as his shoulder protested.

"You ought to have a soak. Brenda's got beans and rice and cornbread ready for whenever." They headed up, Jack grabbing the screen door.

"I'll get Jason settled first. I can wait." His whole body was one big ache, so now or later didn't make no nevermind.

Jason was on the sofa still, eyes closed, fingers opening and closing. Momma was hovering some, staring at Mini like that would do something.

"How's that root beer sitting, Mini? You ready for some cornbread?" There was no way he was gonna go for fake cheer, but he didn't want to be all doom and gloom, either.

"Yeah." Jason reached for him, touched his fingers once. "This is fucked, ain't it?"

"Watch your mouth, son."

"Yes, Momma."

His fingers twitched, wanting to twine with Jason's. "Momma, could you dish up? I'm hurtin' some." There. That got her going, and Bax was able to sit and put a hand on Jason's leg, just resting.

That got Mini to relax, to ease back into the cushions and stop a while. They didn't say anything for a bit, just sat and breathed and ached. Momma brought food, and Bax choked some down, glad to see Jason eat a whole plate of cornbread.

As soon as they were through, Momma started fluttering again, Jason tensing beside him. She went on about towels and sheets and liniment and...

He was fixin' to growl when Jack took her elbow. "The boys'll figure it."

"But."

"Woman, come on to the bed. The boys'll figure it and you can cook in the morning." Jack hauled Momma on out, leaving both him and Jason chuckling.

"You ready for a bath and bed, Mini? I could stand to sleep about a year." He stroked Jason's knee absently, his fingers drawing little barbed wire patterns.

"Yeah, Bax. You. I wouldn't give for you, yeah?"

"I know that, stupid. Same here." He laughed a little, patting Jason's leg before hauling his sore ass up. "Come on, you. If you're nice I'll wash your back."

"I don't get things working again, it won't be worth washing."

"You shut your trap. You don't ever talk like that. You'll get that buckle yet." He pulled Jason up more gently than he wanted to, leading Mini to the bathroom and some steam. It would make them both feel better.

They'd figure it, just like Jack said they would.

The alternative just wasn't anything he'd accept.

Chapter Ten

God, he'd never noticed how many fucking noises this house made in the dark.

Jason sat on the edge of the bed, listening to all the things — from the wind to the snoring to the creaking. It was fucking insane. Really. He couldn't sleep because waking up sucked. He couldn't wander because, even if this was the house he'd grown up in, he didn't know it well enough. He couldn't listen to the TV because that'd wake everybody up.

If he had to sit here until the morning, though, he might lose what was left of his mind.

He still had his jeans on and it only took a few minutes to find his boots. He knew where Bax's truck keys were. He had a good idea where the truck was parked. He'd just go sit and listen to the radio and have a couple of smokes where no one'd scream at him.

It took forever, and he kept his eyes squeezed tight, pretending that if he opened them he could see. He made it down the hallway, fingers dragging on the wallpaper. Then he stumbled a little until he found the back of the sofa, the sofa table behind.

That got him to the kitchen, the floor feeling slick as shit under his feet. He whapped his hip good and hard on the table, the sting enough to make him stop a second, bite back the scream that wanted out of him.

After that, getting the truck keys and getting down the steps was easy.

Of course, finding the truck? Not so much.

Everything was fucked there, from the wind distracting

him to the weird sound of the grass on his jeans to the bugs flying on his bare chest. He was lathered in sweat by the time he hit the fence, and he grabbed a hold of it and just shook it, snarling and cussing under his breath.

Then he fucking turned around and tried again.

God damn it.

Jason didn't have the foggiest fucking idea how long it took, but he finally did it. He found the motherfucking truck, he got the key in the door, climbed in.

And if he had himself a good long scream, complete with pounding the living shit out of the steering wheel before he got the radio going? There wasn't nobody to fucking see it. The radio drowned out everything outside, and Jason could put his head back and pretend he was just waiting for Bax to come on out of the arena, avoiding all the kids who wanted autographs.

Jason sat for a good while. Maybe ten songs. Maybe twenty before the pounding on the driver's window had him jumping out of his skin.

His eyes popped open and he turned to look, that panicky sickness hitting him again. *Fuck.* He scrabbled for the buttons, doors unlocking and locking, the passenger window sliding down and back up before he found the right one. "Whut?"

"Jason? Jesus, Jason, what the fuck are you doing?" Bax's voice sounded different when a man couldn't see that sharp-featured face. Right now it had that added note of panic, too.

"Listening to the radio. Is it morning already?" He wasn't ready to go in yet.

"Well, technically, yeah. It's almost four. I just... I was coming to check on you and you..." Panting. He could hear panting. Bax must've run.

"I'm cool. I couldn't sleep. Go on back to bed, man. I'm just going to sit."

"I cain't just leave you out here, Mini." Bax's fingers stroked his elbow, right where it crooked against the door

60

frame. "Come on. I'll keep you company."

"You got to be tired." Hell, he was tired, and he kept dozing off in the truck.

"A little, yeah." The man didn't back off, though, just tugged at his arm a little. "Come on, Jase. We'll get something munchy and sit and jaw."

He bit back the urge to snap and tell Bax to back the fuck off. Bax was being decent to him and fuck knew, the man'd have to leave in a couple of days for North Carolina. And didn't that ache some?

Shit.

Even when he'd been hurt, he'd gone with.

"Okay. Come on. I'll go back to the bed, let you get some sleep." He'd talk to the doc today—find out how long he was gonna have to wait this out.

"'Kay." Bax waited until he got the truck turned off, got himself on his own two feet. Only then did Bax offer his arm.

Jason took it, telling himself it wasn't for long. It couldn't be. He'd just bumped his fucking head.

Bax led him back the way he'd come out, less the detour to the fence, all the way back to the bedroom, where Bax pushed him right down on the bed and started tugging at his boots, silent as a ghost.

"I can do it." He was going to scream, he could feel it bubbling up in him.

His left boot thumped to the floor, sounding like a fucking bomb hitting ground zero.

"Fine. Fine, Mini. You just go ahead. Sorry I fucking bothered you."

"Don't snarl at me, Bax. Not right now." That was the only warning he was fucking going to give.

"I'm just trying to help," Bax said quietly. "I don't know what else to do."

"Me either." He couldn't fucking do this too long. He'd just put a gun to his head and get it over with.

Sighing, Bax pulled at his other boot, then pushed him

down to wrangle his jeans off. The air felt almost cold against his skin, goosebumps rising up. Bax paused, hands on Jason's knees.

"Right now you need to sleep, Mini. I could stay…if it would make it better.'

"I…" God, he was a girl. "I just keep hearing all these noises, man, and it just… It ain't right."

"Well, that's probably regular enough, when you can't see what they are." The rustle of the sheets was the only sound for a minute, then Bax slid into bed next to him, solid and heavy on the other side of the mattress. "This okay?"

"Yeah." He reached out, needing to know for sure, Bax's arm warm and right and there.

"I got you." Bax's fingers slid up, twined with his. "I got your back."

"Thank God." He couldn't figure it otherwise.

Couldn't even start to.

Chapter Eleven

"Will you quit it!" Bax snarled at Momma, feeling like an idiot for making her look like that, for making Jack stare him down. The fact was he didn't want to go. He just didn't. It hadn't even been two weeks since Jason had gotten hurt, and he wasn't in any place to go ride.

Momma stopped fluttering around with his duffel bag and went to the kitchen, shoulders stiff, and Bax sighed, rolling his neck.

"Shit."

"You got your stuff together, buddy?" Jason was leaning on the door frame, eyes looking like he could see. The doctor'd said it could be days, years, never. Hell, he'd said there might be days that Jason'd see stuff and days Mini couldn't.

"Mostly. I'll be back Monday, early as I can." He was flying instead of driving, not willing to leave Jason that long.

"Tell the guys I'm recovering, yeah? Nothing else." Shit, as if Coke and AJ were gonna handle that. Fucking Coke'd been on the phone two times a day for two weeks, Jason refusing to talk to anybody.

"I'll tell them. They'll pester me." Shit, they'd hold him down and beat him. "You do what the doc says, okay?"

"Yeah, Bax. You keep your mind in the middle and your ass on them bulls."

"I will." It was bullshit, but he'd try. He needed the money. If he could earn enough to sit out a couple of events, all the better.

"Good. Don't let Momma give you shit, you just go on.

I'm managing."

"She wasn't giving the man shit. She was trying to help, and you boys ought to be a bit nicer to her," Jack said, eyeing them both.

Only Jase couldn't see it, so it was up to Bax to hang his head.

Jason, though, he just snarled. "If she's miserable having me here, she can just come on and tell me."

Well, shit.

"Come on, Jason. Walk me to the truck." Hefting one bag and rolling the other, Bax nodded at Jack, who had puffed all up, but was deflating now. They all knew how damned hard this was, and Jason could be a bear when he was hurt.

He waited until they got outside before stopping, letting his bags drop. "It'll be three days, man. I'll be back. And you know your momma's not wanting you gone. She's just scared."

"I know. I'll be here." Jason sighed, squeezed his arm. Fuck, this sucked. "Good ride, man."

"Thanks, Mini." The urge to kiss the man goodbye shocked him, and Bax settled for a quick, hard hug before he backed off. "You got the path back in okay?"

"Yeah." Jason waved once, then turned around, moving slow and careful, looking old all of the sudden.

Goddamn it all.

Bax tossed his shit in the truck, punching the back bumper hard, cussing under his breath. He didn't want to leave Jason behind. Not one bit. But he had to ride.

* * * *

The drive to the airport and all the shit to get his gear through security passed in a blur and Bax slept all the way to North Carolina, determined to stop thinking, even if for just a few hours.

And it was just his fucking luck to meet up with Nate and Coke and AJ in the line for the hotel shuttle.

"Andy!" Coke grabbed his arm, frowning up at him. "What the fuck is going on with Jason?"

Asshole, thinking he could just get to know because... Oh, hell. Coke thought Mini fucking hung the moon.

"He's banged up, man. Needs a few weeks off." There. That was all he was allowed to tell. Officially.

"Uh-huh." Coke's lips twisted, those gray eyes staring him down. "You tell him that if he needs anything, anything at all, call, yeah?"

AJ nodded, bouncing like a jack in the box. "You know it, Andy. We got y'all's backs."

"Hey, you."

Oh, yay. The gang was all here.

Nate chuckled, clapping him on the back. "I bet you're sick of people asking, huh?"

He just shook his head. "I just want him back on tour."

He got three somber nods, then another couple of guys coming over, worried and offering help. Jesus, it was good to know and deeply fucked, all at once.

Bax finally broke free of everyone but Coke at the hotel, smiling and nodding until he figured his face might crack. Damn.

"C'mon, cowboy. I'll buy you a beer. You look like you need one."

"You gonna badger me about Jason?" He wanted that beer, but he sure couldn't take anymore hard poking. He stared right into Coke's eyes, serious as a heart attack.

"Nope. I'm gonna gossip with you about Kynan and them Brazilian boys and possibly tell you a terrible joke we heard last week." That rough hand took his elbow, Coke moving careful-like toward the bar.

"How're you, old man? I hear you took a Hell of a shot in Orlando." Coke was the oldest bullfighter on tour. And the best. Like Old Faithful.

"Shee-it. I look like I went forty-two rounds with Mike Tyson. Good thing I got high-necked shirts." Gramps couldn't turn his head, his neck'd been broken so many times.

"Yeah. I hear you. My shoulder felt like it was gonna pop right out when I got on a couple practice bulls Tuesday." 'Course, he'd slid right past his own appointment with Doc.

"Hell gettin' old, Andy." Coke settled down, motioned to the bartender. "Still, it's better than the alternative. You hear that Houston Rogers is out for the season? He popped his hip."

"No shit?" Man, the bulls were getting stronger every damned year. And they were getting hammered by the big monsters. "Man, he wasn't in the money, but he wasn't fixin' to get sent down or nothin'."

Coke nodded, his whole upper body moving as he did. "And his woman's expecting."

"Lord." Well, they'd do some sort of relief auction for him. Hell, he'd bet Beau Lafitte, the current world champ, would donate a vest or something, make Houston a chunk of change.

"Yeah. He'll be back next year, right as rain. Rookie's got Bell's luck, you know?" No shit—Sam Bell couldn't get a good run for love or money.

"How'd they do last week? Sam and Beau?" Jason and Beau had been tight for a long while, but had gone their separate ways for whatever reason. Bax never asked.

"Beau rode for a ninety-three pointer on Greenhorn in the short go. Sam won a little money in round two, so it wasn't all bad for him."

They got their beers, both drinking deep.

"Oh, that's hitting the spot," Bax said, smiling over. Coke was quiet, easy. Not so chatty that Bax wanted to take his teeth out.

"Yep. You wantin' food, man? They got bar stuff. I'm wantin' a burger."

"I'd kill for a steak. I've had beans and cornbread till I cain't." Bless Momma's heart. She must have stock in pork products.

"Missus Scott is known for that, man." Coke raised a

hand. "Honey, I need a menu and another round."

Bax almost turned down the beer, but he didn't have to ride until tomorrow at eight, and God knew he could get over anything by then.

They set to talking shop—bullshitting about bulls and riders, about the contractors and the new bonus money coming down the pike. Normal shit. Shit that made it normal and easy. They ordered steaks and salads and potatoes.

Bax sucked down his third beer, leaning his elbows on the table after the little gal took the salad plate away. "You know, this is the best I've felt in a couple weeks."

"I bet. It's weird, being off the circuit like that."

"Oh, I'm okay. I mean, for me. It's Jase I'm missing. He's got me worried." Somewhere in the back of his head he knew he wasn't supposed to talk on this shit, but Coke would find out. He always did.

"What can I do, Andy? You know y'all are dear to me."

"I don't know. We'll just have to see how he heals up." If Jason healed up. Bax didn't even want to think what would happen if the man never could see again.

"You just let me know. He's... His head's okay, ain't it? He ain't...broke-broke."

"He cain't see, Coke." Half whispering, Bax rested his cheek on his palm, shuddering just to think of it. "He's got some kind of pressure."

"Oh, shit." Coke closed his eyes a second, the look pure hurt. "Oh, Jesus, Andy. Is it... I mean, is it all gone?"

"They say his eyes are fine. Like workable." Sipping his beer, Bax stared at the table. "But he's got this thing. It could come back tomorrow. It might never."

"Don't you tell anybody, Andy. Not a soul until after the season's over." Coke's hand landed on his wrist, gnarled fingers hard as hell. "Those sponsors'll leave him like rats off a sinking ship and he just signed that soda pop one."

"I know that. Hell, I wasn't even supposed to tell you, and you like him. But you always know." Bax blinked, looking at his fourth empty. "You'd best walk me to my room."

"Yeah, okay. You don't worry 'bout telling me, Andy. Shit, you can't shoulder your shit and Jason's all alone. Man needs friends."

"I'm glad he's got you." He stood, swaying, remembering all the damned Dramamine he'd taken. "Think I might be sick, Coke. Watch your boots."

"Easy. Easy, now. Gimme your key." A bottle of cold water was pushed in his hand, seemingly out of nowhere.

"Thanks." Fumbling, he hauled out his key, handing it over. Shit, drunk like a cheap floozie on Mad Dog or something. He was getting old.

"Drink the water." Those strong old arms muscled him into the room just like they'd pushed him out of bulls' ways, around arenas.

"I will. Promise." If he could get it open. This was what happened when Jase wasn't around to take care of him.

Coke wasn't near as good at it, but the man managed, getting him naked and watered and in the bed, the TV on for light. "Sleep, Andy. We're having breakfast at nine thirty. You come down."

"I will," he mumbled, curling into the comforter. "Need to call Jase."

"Mmmhmm." That rough hand rubbed his back a second. "Lay your burden down, Andy. I'll carry it for one night."

"You're the savior, man. In or out of the arena." Bax settled in, letting the water fix his drunken brain, and he was asleep before he even knew whether Coke stayed or went. Bax was ready to let it go. Just for one night.

68

Chapter Twelve

"Jason? Honey? You want to watch Andy ride? It's coming on the TV."

Yeah. Yeah, he wanted to. It wasn't fucking happening, though, was it? "No, Momma. You just pay attention, tell me how he did."

The bedroom door was locked and it was going to stay that way. He had a bottle of Jack, he had music on the CD player — he was settled.

Two weekends Bax'd come and gone, but then the travel had gotten too expensive and too tiring and he'd told Bax to just go on and work.

"Son, you can't just stay in there."

He heard the doorknob rattle and he sighed. Yeah. Yeah, he could. He could sit in here and drink himself asleep. He could see in his dreams, just clear as day.

"Go root for Bax, Momma. He needs a good ride before the break."

"He does. But he needs you rooting for him, too. You get your ass out here." Now Momma was using the mother voice.

"I am rooting for him. Leave me be, Momma." He wasn't eight anymore.

"Damn it, Jason, I'm worried about you. Come have some coffee and cake with me and Jack." From demanding to pleading, she had it all.

"I'll have breakfast with you. Bax'll be calling after a while. There's a tape delay." He couldn't listen to all those guys living his life. He just couldn't.

"Okay, honey. Call if you need me." She finally left

him, just the sound of George and the ticking of the clock sounding now.

He poured himself another round, jonesing on the burn. Every so often he thought he saw a color, a shape. No light, but there was something there.

His cell finally rang maybe an hour later, buzzing right next to his hand, making his butt vibrate.

"'Lo?" If it wasn't Bax, he'd just hang up.

"Jason! Is that you man? It's AJ. Bax said to call."

Oh. Now Bax couldn't even bother to call him personally. "Did he ride?"

"Yeah eighty three and a half. But... Well..." AJ trailed off, saying something to someone in the background.

"But what! Goddamn it! AJ! What the fuck happened to him?" He stood up in a rush, knocking all sorts of shit over as he headed for the door.

"He's in sports medicine. We don't know for sure how bad he's broke up, Jase, but something in his leg snapped." AJ sounded like he was just plumb worried.

"Jesus fucking Christ. Okay. Okay, you call me soon as you hear something. I'll..."

He'd what?

Ride to the fucking rescue?

He shut the phone with a snap, growling as he stumbled, slammed into the door. "Momma! Momma! Bax is hurt!"

"Well, open the door, you fool man." Momma was whacking on the other side of the door, calling him names.

"I'm fucking trying!" His Goddamn head was swimming, but he finally got it, yanking the door open. "His leg snapped. AJ called."

"Oh. Oh, well, damn it all." Momma grabbed his arm, pulling him along to the front room. "Jack! Jack, we need to find out where they'll take Andy for x-rays."

"Y'all'll have to go get him and bring him home." He stumbled along behind her.

"Jesus fuck, Jason. You look like shit."

"Fuck you, Jack. That doesn't matter."

"We can't leave you here." Jack took hold of him, leaving Momma to run amok and get shit together.

"You sure as shit can. I'll be fine." He was a grown man, goddamn it.

"Jason, don't be stupid. Andy will be asking for you." Momma was all over, her voice bouncing crazily.

"I can't go. Sports medicine'll be all over. You just go get him." He couldn't let anybody know.

"I'll stay here, then. Jack, you go get Andy and bring him home. Everyone knows I hate to travel."

His phone rang again, cutting off Momma's last word.

"'Lo? Bax?"

"Hey, Mini." Oh. Hell, yes. It was Bax. "You okay? AJ didn't rile you all up, did he?"

"I'm sending Momma and Jack to get you."

"Oh, now. I'll be..." He heard the sharp indrawn breath, the harder curse word Bax spat out. "Goddamn it, Shaun, would you quit poking!"

Shaun was one of the best sports medicine assistants around. Looked as if Bax wasn't on his way to the ER yet.

"What happened?" He sort of spun a second, Jack leading him over to a chair.

"Oh, shit, Mini. I got hung up between the bull and the fence. You know how it is. He caught my leg." Bax swallowed, the sound a dry click, then chuckled. "It's all pointy."

"They going to have to cast it up or surge on it?" Fuck, he should be there. He should be helping.

"I dunno. They're wanting to give me the good drugs now, but I wanted to talk to you. Make sure you were good. If I have to get surgery, I'll come home and have it done." Yeah. Yeah, Bax hated the big hospitals with a passion.

"I'll send family to get you. I should be there."

"It's... It's okay, Jase. We can be all roughed up together, huh?" Bax got to laughing, the sound adrenaline fueled, a little crazy. Just like always.

"Yeah, yeah. You let Shaun and them work on you.

Momma'll be there in a few hours." Where the fuck was Bax, anyway?

He got grunt, low and guttural, the sound one he damned well knew. Bax in pain. Then he heard a clacking and shuffling. "Jason? It's Coke, man. They're moving him. He sat back here through the rest of the short go, the damned fool. You tell your folks to stay put. I'll bring him on home. Been wanting to see you anyway."

"Coke?" He swayed, queasy as hell. "You don't let them cut him open there."

"Don't think he'll need it. I've seen enough to know. You cowboy up, son. I'll bring him home. He'll be fine." Yeah. Yeah, okay, he could count on Coke. He might could even stand Coke to see him. Maybe.

"Thanks, man. I'll have Momma pick y'all up in Abilene. Tell him... Tell him we're waiting."

"No need. I got Bax's truck, and I will. It helped him, Jason. Talking to you. He's missing you bad. I'll talk to you soon." The phone went dead, leaving him sitting there, listening to nothing.

"Coke's bringing him home."

He heard Momma's sigh. "He's a good man. You just let me know when, son. Jack, we need to get Jason some water."

"I'm fine, Momma."

"Uh-huh. Water." Nagging old woman. He did love her.

"Here you go, son." Jack was solid, salt of the earth, and completely whipped.

"Thanks, Jack." He hunted the glass a second, but got it, only spilling a little. "Coke says it doesn't look like surgery."

Coke said talking to him had helped.

"Well, that old fart has seen more riders come down the pike than most." Jack clapped him on the back, and momma put something food-y into his other hand, and he just sat and tried not to think on Bax hurtin'.

Tried not to think on how a damned fine year was turning into something... Something else.

Chapter Thirteen

Bax woke up when the truck stopped. He sat in the back seat, his leg stretched out longways on the seat, the cast all propped on pillows. Lord, he was groggy and his mouth tasted like cotton.

Stupid fucking bull. Stupid fucking leg. At least he'd won the event, covering all three bulls with a high score of eighty nine.

"Coke? We're home, right? I'm not hallucinating?" God, his voice sounded like shit.

"No, son. We're at Miss Scott's."

They pulled in, Momma and Jack pouring out of the house, Momma wrenching the car door open and looking at him.

"Andy. Son. Lord, you worried me. So glad you're home."

"Hi, Momma." Oh, she looked tired. About as tired as he felt. Poor Brenda.

"What did the Doc say? Are you hungry? I made y'all supper. Coke, honey, you'll eat chicken and dumplings, won't you?"

"Yes, ma'am. How's Jase?"

Momma's face fell and she shook her head, lips tight.

"That good, huh? Well, help me inside, so I can see for myself." He'd gotten crutches, but the Doc didn't even want him using those for nearly two weeks because of the shoulder he'd separated the night Jason gotten hurt.

"Sure, honey." She reached for him, and he heard the sound of a swat.

"Woman, last thing we need is you hurtin' yourself. Let me and Mr. Coke do it."

Momma's eyes went wide and she blushed.

Dark.

Well, well.

Bax blushed a little, too, not wanting to think on that too much. He let Coke and Jack haul him out, carrying him easily to the house. Strong old bastards.

"Mini! Where in Hell are you?"

Jack sighed, shook his head. "Pro'bly sleeping off another drunk. He ain't been real jolly."

"Well, he can get his unjolly ass out here," Bax growled before raising his voice to a bellow. "*Jason!*"

"Whut? Bax?" Jason stumbled out of the middle bedroom, looking like hammered shit. Mini hadn't shaved, was about gray, and was skinny as if he hadn't eaten in a month. "Bax?"

"Yeah. They put me on the couch. Come on over and say hey." Damn it. Nobody better help Jason come to him.

"You come by yourself?"

"No. No, Jase. I brought him home." Coke sighed as Jason stepped back. "Jase, buddy. I know, okay? Come see Andy."

Jason swayed a half second, then Mini slunk down the hallway, heading for him, slow and careful.

Jesus, it near broke his heart. But Bax hurt too bad to let the sympathy get to him. He wanted to have Jason close enough to touch.

"Hey, man. How's the leg?" Mini got there, hand on the back of the couch. "Doc say anything?"

"I'm out for the season. It was fairly clean, but it will take six to eight weeks just to get the cast off." He reached right up with his good hand, patting Jason's arm. It eased him.

"Damn." Jason looked down at him, then those poor eyes moved away, just like that. "You hurtin'?"

"Andy, Mr. Coke. You want me to fix y'all some plates?" Momma wouldn't even give Jason a glance.

"That'd be nice, ma'am," Coke said, hauling Jack out of the room. Leaving them alone.

"I got my foot up on a stool. Come sit with me, Mini."

"Momma said you won the round." Jason came around, sat carefully, hand sliding over to him like it was searching him out.

"I did. I didn't win the short go, with an eighty three, but I was the only one to cover all of them." He bit back all of the things he wanted to say about how Jason looked, about how skinny he was. "You been up to no good?"

"Just been here. You... I guess you told Coke?"

"Yeah. He's... Well, Hell, Jase. You know Coke. He's not human." The man could make you tell him the combination to your sister's chastity belt.

It was a relief to see Mini grin, nod. "No. He'd make one hell of a spy or something. A priest."

They both snorted. Jesus, a bullfighter in a collar.

"Hey, that's it," Bax said, patting Jason's hand. "He's the Cowboy Confessor."

"Yeah." Jason's face went still again, and he ducked his head. "Sorry about the leg, man. You were riding good."

"Well, I was good enough to get in for next season." He wasn't sorry. He'd been missing Jason like a sore tooth. "Mini, you look like Hell."

"Yeah? Good thing I don't have to worry about that."

"Fuck you. I got to look at you, don't I? I like the way you look healthy. A lot." Jason couldn't see him blush, at least.

"Yeah." Jason sighed, rubbed his forehead. "I go tomorrow for another CAT scan to look at the swelling."

"Well, that's good, right?" That might mean the swelling was going down. "I missed you, Mini."

"Yeah. It was weird, not going with."

"I bet. I swear to God, I kept waking up, looking for you." Okay, enough sap. No, really.

Jason squeezed his hand hard, then nodded. "I hear you. I... I reckon it's like anything else. Hopefully you won't have to get used to it."

"There you go." They just sat there, shoulder to shoulder, holding hands, until he started dozing off. Well, until he woke up, drooling on Jason's shoulder.

"Come on, son. You need to eat and take another pill." Momma was there, a plate of chicken and dumplings for him. "Coke can take the bed in the guest room. I'll let you have my…"

Jason grunted, waved his hand. "He'll be fine in my room, Momma."

"I will." He didn't want to stay anywhere else. "I just… I'm sorry, y'all. They gave me all those pills."

"It's cool, Bax. Come on. Eat whatever she made you and you can nap."

Momma looked over at Jason, shaking her head. "You could have some, too, son."

"No, Momma. I'm not hungry."

"Eat with me, Jase. Just a little, huh?" Chicken and dumplings. Lord, Momma was going all out, trying to get Jason to eat. "There's a biscuit here."

Jason waved him off. "Nah. I'm not in the mood, man. Later, Momma. I promise."

"Bullshit. You're going to starve. Just because you got embarrassed with—"

"That's enough, Momma."

"Don't you snap at me."

"Then quit fucking nagging, Momma!" Jason growled, stood up. "I said I wasn't hungry. I'm not a fucking kid. I know when to eat."

"Then why won't you?" Momma was crying now, tears just sliding down her face. "Andy, he won't eat. He got all messed up with the silverware and the plate and not being able to see and—"

"Momma!" Jason was fucking fixing to lose it.

Bax tried to struggle to his feet…foot. Whatever. "Momma, you're a good woman. Putting up with him. Go on and have a sit with Jack and relax a minute. Jason, you get your ass back here and help me to your room." He wasn't gonna let Jase wander off, fists all clenched.

"Isn't that the blind leading the fucking gimpy?"

Someone was gonna lose it. It might not be him, the way

76

Jack and Coke were just staring at them with stony faces. "Mini, please. I need to lie down and I need to just talk with you a bit. Come on."

Jason closed his eyes, throat working, and Bax could see him counting, calming himself down, settling his shit. "Okay. Okay, Bax. You gotta tell me what you need."

"Come over here." He held out his hand so Jason could catch it, then he reeled Jase in. "Now get over here on this side so I can lean. Kinda like New Orleans. You remember that ride?"

He got a grin that just stunned him for the few seconds it lasted. "Yeah. C'mon." Jason settled under his arm, stood strong for him.

That was more like it. "Okay, so. Turn right, yeah?" Slow and steady. They could do it. Jason had fine legs, he had good eyes.

"Tell me they ain't all staring at me, Bax. I'm so fucking tired of being a freak."

"Nope. They all went to the kitchen." They had, when he'd waved them all off. Hell, he knew what Jason meant, and he'd only been laid up a few days. Working slow but sure, they made their way to the hall. "Right a little."

He could feel Mini relax under his arm, move easier. That was it. Just like that. Everyone just needed to stop freaking out and trying to baby the man. It took him getting all bent and mangled for Bax to get that, though. So he could hardly blame Momma.

"Okay, now, we have to turn sideways to get through the door. Swing to your left and step to the side three times." One, two, three... It was a weird, shuffly waltz.

Jason snorted a little, but listened, drawing him into the room. Jesus. How many fucking bottles of booze could Jason drink? They were fucking everywhere.

Bax considered it kind of a triumph when he got settled on the bed, his leg up and a pillow tucked under it. "You've been hittin' the sauce hard, Mini."

"Yep." Jason didn't even apologize for it.

"Well. I ain't gonna bitch, I suppose. But it makes me worry." There. He'd shut up now, but damn.

"It's better than thinking, Bax. It ain't like I'm driving." The bark of laughter was all hurt. "Tell me about your rides."

"Come and sit, instead of standing there like a stranger." He wanted to hold on to Jason. To feel him, right there and solid and warm. Crazy as it was.

Jason came over right close, scooting up to his side. "You holler if I'm crowding you."

"Not a bit." Resettling his leg, Bax looped an arm around Jason's back, loving the man for all he was worth. "I did good the first ride. Right in the middle the whole way."

"I bet the crowd was going nuts. They love you, man."

"It was good. I edged Beau out for the round. The second ride I did okay, but Baltazar Silva won the go-round. It was the short go that did me in." Damn, the sound of his own leg snapping had been gross.

"Beau's number one now, huh?" Jason and Beau'd been good friends. Real good friends. Once.

"Yeah. He's pushing hard. Gonna make a run on it, I think." He stroked the line of Jason's spine, up and down, not even thinking about it.

"Yeah. I... I been doing a lot of thinking, Bax, about what I'm gonna do if they tell me the swelling's all gone down tomorrow."

His throat tightened up, fear making ice slide down his back. "Yeah? What's that?"

Those eyes shot over to him, sure as shit seeming as if they were looking right at him. "I'm gonna need you to take care of Momma. She's gonna marry Jack, I think."

No. Oh, Hell no.

"Jase. That's crazy talk. We'll figure it." He tightened his grip when Jason would have pulled away. "Call me selfish, but no way."

"I ain't living like this. I can't cowboy up, I can't ride, I can't fucking drive my truck. Shit, Bax. What am I gonna do? Have Momma take care of me my whole life? I can't even shave."

"You have to give it some time, Jason." *Shit. Oh, Jesus.* He was gonna break down and bawl. "I cain't know what it feels like, I know it. But I need you, man."

"Shit. You did good without me. I heard." Jason grinned at him. "Hard-assed cowboy."

Bax grinned back, even though Jase couldn't see him. "I was riding hard to get a few weekends off. So I could come see you."

"I want to see you." The words were bit out, just near growled. "More than— Fuck. I do."

"I want that, too, Mini." Bax swallowed hard, trying to get the lump out of his throat. "I been wanting all sorts of..." Fuck. Now wasn't the time, was it?

Jason nodded, squeezed his hand. "Yeah, and we ain't never had half a chance and now we're both broke dick."

"Broke something." He had to laugh. Just a little. What the Hell else could he do? "Just promise me you'll talk with me on it before you do nothin'."

"You got my word, buddy. I ain't looking to cause no big thing."

No big thing. Jesus fuck.

Bax leaned a little, not really snuggling. Not really. "Rest with me a bit. You ain't gonna hurt me."

"You need a pill or something?" Jason's hand was moving like it had a mind of its own, petting his arm in long, slow strokes.

"No. No, I'm good." His leg ached like crazy, but he didn't want either of them to move. And God knew he lived with hurt all the time. "This is fine. Just fine."

"'Kay." Jason nodded, leaned right back. "Glad you're home, Bax."

"Me, too, Mini. Me, too." He was. More than Jason would ever know.

Looked like he'd gotten home just in time.

Chapter Fourteen

Momma took him home and helped him up to the door. He didn't wait to listen to her tell them all the lies he'd told her. The swelling was gone. He had some sight on the edges, enough to see light versus dark, to see some shapes, but that was all she wrote.

The fucking doctor'd offered him a cane.

A cane.

Him.

So he'd told Momma there was still a chance and had her bring his sorry ass home.

He locked his door behind him and found a bottle, taking a hard swig, letting the burn wear the edges off the hole that was left in him. Jason'd spent last night holding Bax and praying—praying hard. He just needed another chance, a chance to get out there and ride. A chance to cowboy up.

Didn't look like he was fixin' to get it, though. Goddamn it.

Didn't look like Bax was wanting to go easy on him, neither, which didn't make no sense. They'd put down a dog, a blind calf, and call it humane. Another shot of the bottle and he set to wandering, pacing his room—six steps this way, four steps that and around the end of the bed to the window.

The pounding on his door started up not long after that, but it wasn't Momma or Jack. It was Bax hollering. "Mini. Let me in."

"You're 'sposed to be off that foot."

Pushy cowboy.

"So let me in so I can sit down, fool man. Bad enough I

80

couldn't go with you—" Another thump sounded, then a yelp and a crash.

Oh, for fuck's sake.

"Goddamn it, be careful, Bax!" He wrenched the door open, arms flailing, head turned as he tried his damnedest to see something.

"I'm all right. Down here." Something tapped his ankle, maybe that damned crutch Bax wasn't even supposed to be using yet. "Need some help, though. Take like, three steps to your right."

It was kinda funny how Bax had just fallen right in to helping him, being his eyes. That part seemed to come easily. Weird, but it worked.

"I got you." He headed over and reached down. "Lord, Bax. You're gonna regret that in the morning." Jason got his hands under Bax's arms, pulled him up, sure and steady.

"I regret it now. What the fuck is with the morning?" He could hear that stupid grin, though, knew that sharp face would just be split with it. Bax's good arm wrapped around his neck, and they did the dance of shuffle to the bedroom.

"You want the bed?" They managed okay, better than, maybe. Damn, Bax felt fine against him.

"I do." Huffing a little, Bax plopped down on the bed, hand sliding down to tug at his wrist. "Okay. Tell me."

He closed his eyes—it was harder, lying to Bax. "I got to just wait still."

"Don't you do that. Don't you bullshit me, Jason. I know you better than anyone." Bax's fingers bit into his skin, Andy leaning close.

He gritted his teeth, took a deep, deep breath to calm himself down. *Oh. Oh, damn.* He could smell Bax. Christ, he'd know that scent anywhere—a weird mixture of leather and smell good and grass and horse.

That good arm wrapped around him, Bax's short-short hair brushing his cheek. "Come on, Jason. I can help carry the damned load."

"It's over, Bax. All of it. I got just a little, on the edges.

81

That's all."

He could feel the sharp, indrawn breath, could hear the little groan Bax tried to stifle. "Jesus, Mini. I... We'll figure it. A little is better than nothing, and that means it might come back."

"I didn't tell Momma." He stood up, walked away to the window, let the sun bake him a little. "You know I see just fine when I'm dreaming?"

"Well, honey, you're hurt, not stupid."

That tickled him, down deep, and he started laughing, just hooting with it. The sounds went on and on even if, in the end, there wasn't any humor in it.

"Come and sit, Jason."

Yeah. Okay, yeah. Bax couldn't come to him.

Jason nodded, headed over to sit on the bed, head down. "I'm real sorry, cowboy."

"For what? You didn't do a Goddamned thing wrong. Shit, Mini, you had that ride in the bag." Bax touched him again, barely there at first, then stronger, those lean fingers tracing patterns on his leg. He could see those hands in his head, scarred and brown and so damned pretty.

"Yeah." Still, he was sorry about all the shit he was fixin' to miss. He should've died in the arena, just right then on that bull.

"Come here." Oh, it felt good when Bax pulled him down, settling him on the opposite side of that bad leg. The man didn't say nothin' else, just held onto him. He leaned good and hard, fingers squeezing the comforter tight.

"Don't give up on me yet," Bax whispered, pushing in close, hands gripping him, not the covers.

"It ain't you that's ruint, Andy." He reached out, needing to feel something good, so badly.

They got all wrapped up together, Bax's bad leg the only thing not curled against him. That cast kinda made it awkward, but Bax didn't seem to care. "You're not out of my game, Mini."

"I ain't no good to you like this. I cain't even pull your

rope."

"Shh. Stop. Just…" Rocking against him a little, Bax held on, all but crawling right into him.

Damn. Just damn.

He groaned, pushing closer, cock doing its damnedest to fill up. "Bax…"

Rough fingers brushed over his cheek, catching on the stubble there, before tracing his mouth. "I got you."

"I…" His heart stopped as he slid tongue his out to taste those calluses.

Oh. Oh, sweet Christ. Please.

There was a moment of complete silence, as if the whole fucking world was holding its breath. Then Bax shifted, pulled, and Jason pressed his mouth against the softest, hottest lips he'd ever tasted. His hands cupped Bax's face, and both of them were just breathing together, lips together, moving so slow. Hand sliding around to flatten against the back of his neck, Bax gave it up for him, opening right up to let him taste. Jesus, he'd been dreaming about this too damned long.

Oh. Oh, yeah. He dipped his tongue in, taking what Bax was offering, just in case. It was the hottest thing he'd ever done, ever.

Panting, Bax pressed against him, pushing a little. Oh, nothing fast or fierce. But those sounds had to be happy ones. Jason took his chance, one hand moving south, sliding down that belly. Hard. Those fine muscles were so hard.

"Oh…" The sound came on a single breath, Bax shuddering for him, pushing up into his touch. "Jase…"

"Tell me it's okay." He rested his forehead against Bax's, needing to touch so bad.

"God, yes. It's fucking okay." Bax reached with him, pushing his hand down, right there. "Christ."

"Bax." Oh. Oh, shit. Hard. Hot. He slid his thumb all the way along the shaft, his fingers curling to feel Bax's balls.

"Jase." The back of Bax's hand rubbed right up against his own zipper, pressing it back against his cock, giving him some maddening friction.

It was a little messy, but he found Bax's lips again, this kiss less tender, more sharp and toothy.

Bax started humping against his hand as best as Andy could with one leg in a cast, and damned if that grumpy bastard didn't cuss him when he didn't move fast enough to get more of the touching going.

"Bossy fucker." He worked at Bax's fly, hunting skin. "Always pushing me."

"Always need pushing."

When the sweet dick finally popped out into his hand it was like Christmas. Oh, he'd seen it, but this... This was all heat and damp and fucking beautiful to his fingers.

"Bax. Bax..." He could feel Bax's pulse, right in his hand. His thumb slid over the ridge at the tip, the skin there slick, a wee bit bumpy.

Struggling a little, Bax tried to get into his jeans, grunting every time his thumb moved on that amazing skin. "Jason. Gonna explode. I swear to God. Been waiting so long."

"I can... Shit, Bax. I can smell you. Makes my damn mouth water." He couldn't fucking catch his breath, couldn't think, couldn't do a damn thing but touch and feel right now.

"Fuck, Jase. I need." Yeah. Yeah, he could feel it in the desperate touch, the way Bax's body moved restlessly against him.

It was easy, to just grab hold and work that heavy cock, jack Bax off, give the man what he needed. The muscles of Bax's belly quivered against his arm, the one good leg moving heavily against his hip as Bax moaned and thrashed. Andy was on fire for him.

"Come on. Come on now, I got you." Right now. He had the fine son of a bitch.

"Jason!" That was it. He thought he could smell Bax before? When the fine son of a bitch came over his hand it was pure overload. His whole body shuddered and he squeezed his eyes shut tight. Fuck, he'd waited. It was so fucking hot. So good.

"Kiss me, Mini." Bax's nose banged right into his, but they got it going, got the kiss hard and deep just about the time Bax got a hold of his dick.

Oh. Oh, fuck. Yes. Please. He... Right fucking there.

There wasn't anything wrong with his body and he scrambled closer, hips fucking Bax's hand like there was no tomorrow.

"Christ. Jason. You... Hot." Looked like Bax was all babbling, too. Andy got him in a firm grip, rubbing up and down, squeezing top to bottom.

He could feel his orgasm crawling right up his spine, settling in the base of his skull, lights firing off in his eyes. *Oh. Oh, fuck. Yes.* His teeth rattled, he shot so hard, the release of pressure almost painful.

"Sweet. Jesus, Jase, you're so fucking good." Bax kissed him again, sloppier than ever, almost lazy. Uncoordinated.

"I." He didn't know what to say, so he didn't. He just held on.

"Mmmhmm. Me too." Bax wrapped right around him, grunting when his cast thumped against the bed. "Here, just turn here... Yeah."

They got settled, sinking into the bed.

For the first time in weeks, Jason just smiled and slept, not scared of his dreams.

Chapter Fifteen

Bax left Jason sleeping.

That was harder than it sounded, considering the damned cast and all, but Bax did it, mainly so he could clear out all the whiskey bottles. He met Momma in the kitchen, smiling a little when she gave him the official worried look. "He's sleeping."

"Real sleep? Thank God. Did he tell you the truth, Andy?"

"He'll tell you when he's ready, Momma. Just give him time." That might keep her from poking. "I'm starving."

"Sure, son. You want burgers? I think I got the meat out." Oh, Christ. She was fixin' to just lose it and he couldn't blame her, not with Jason like he'd been.

Bax teetered over and gave her a big old hug, squeezing tight "You know what? I think you ought to go have a shower and get Jack to take you out to supper."

"That ain't gonna get you and Coke fed, honey." Momma holding on for a long minute. "I'm scared for him, Andy. I'm real scared. He... He's given up. What's he gonna do?"

"Ma'am, you don't need to worry on that right this second, either the food or your son. Me and Andy, we'll figure it." Coke wandered in, headed straight for the fridge as if he lived there.

Bax stared at Gramps a moment, half smiling. Coke was like no one else he knew. "He's got the right of it. Coke can cook a burger. What you need is a night out. Now, go get your man."

"You. Y'all'll watch him?" Man, Momma wasn't as dumb as Jason thought.

Coke nodded, and Bax patted her back. "We will, Momma.

I made him promise... Well, we made a deal. It'll be okay."

"Okay. Okay, me and Jack'll go have bite, maybe a beer. There's beers for y'all in the porch fridge. Burger fixin's. Don't go buy him any whiskey."

"Nope. No whiskey." Mini needed to sober up.

"Good boy." She kissed his cheek, nodded to Coke then headed into the front room, Jack waiting on her.

"Lord, this is a mess." Coke started digging out food. "Sit, Andy, 'fore you fall."

"Thanks." The little stool by the counter was just the right height to slump on, and Bax waited until the door clicked shut behind Momma and Jack before he glanced over at Coke. "He's fixing to do something really stupid, Coke."

Coke looked over at him, eyebrow arched. "What're you saying, Andy?"

"I'm saying he asked me to take care of Momma for him, Coke." Jesus, just saying that out loud made him queasy.

Coke went about gray, the pickle jar creaking in his fist. "No. No, that ain't how this is gonna work, Andy."

"Well, he's thinking he's done. So what are we gonna do?" Thank God someone else was with him on this. Momma was just too upset, and she'd let Jase walk on her because he was her baby. Coke would help him.

"Who says he has to be done?" The pickles got set down, Coke staring straight at him.

Bax almost fell off the stool. "He cain't see, Coke."

"So? He ain't used his eyes for nothing more than getting away from the bulls. That's why I'm there."

His mouth just dropped right open, and he stared at Coke as if the man had two heads. "But you... I... That's crazy." Wasn't it?

"Crazy? Crazier than watching him drink himself to death? Or put a bullet in his head?" Coke shook his head. "Shit, Andy. It'll take time. Have him tell the fucking sponsors he's hurt bad, needs a year off, and we'll fucking train him to do this."

Even while he was thinking of ways to tell Coke he was

crazier than a bedbug, a little spark of hope lit up his belly. "You really think he can? I mean, I know he's ridden bulls more than once with his eyes closed."

"It'll take time. We got time." Coke came right up close, staring at him. "Shit, Andy, if it don't work, if it can't, it'll give him something to hope for. Something to believe in till we can figure him something else."

Nodding, he held out his hand. "Shake on it. That way I know you mean it, Coke. I cain't lose him."

"No. We ain't giving up on him, Andy." Coke's hand slapped into his, solid and sure as fuck. "He didn't ride with his eyes, Andy. He ain't lost, goddamn it."

Bax decided to believe Coke. Right then and there. And Lord knew he believed in Jason. "Then we'll do it. Not here, though. It will be too hard on Momma."

"No. No, we'll need to make us a plan, yeah? That'll take a bit." Coke stared him down. "The doc didn't say he was gonna get better, did he?"

"No. He said all the swelling was gone. He can maybe see a little. Shapes, that kind of shit." The look on Jason's face had all but broke him.

"Okay. Okay, so we know." Coke closed his eyes, took a deep breath and Bax knew the man was praying. Gramps was a true believer, no matter what anyone said. "We'll have to tell Nate and we'll need to find a place for him to train, to ride again. Somebody close that won't say shit to the money men."

"AJ." It popped out before he even thought, but Aje had the ranch. Had the young bucking bulls. "You know he worships Jase."

Coke tilted his head, lips pursed. "He's got that huge spread, out in the middle of nowhere. Y'all'd know if the press was out and about."

"Yep. And all those rug rats are homeschooled. So even when school's in again we ain't got to worry. Missy loves the way he is with Benji, too." AJ would do it. So would Nate. They were both good 'uns.

Coke nodded. "I got three weeks before the next event. Missus Scott says I can stay a bit. I'll make some calls."

"Are you gonna tell him with me? He'll never believe just me." Not that Jase didn't trust him, but he knew how hard it was to hope.

"There ain't no telling with that stubborn fucker." Coke grinned, shook his head. "We're just gonna do it, Andy. We're not giving him a choice."

"There you go." He felt as if a huge weight had been lifted off, even as he reached for Coke's arm to pull himself up and go check on Jase. Hell, if it didn't work, well...

It was better than just giving up, wasn't it?

Chapter Sixteen

Jesus. What a fucking dream.

Touching Bax.

Touching Bax.

Jason chuckled a little, rolling up in the mattress, rubbing his eyes.

Wait.

Wait, he hadn't seen Bax.

Not even a little.

He saw in his dreams.

He just sat there in the bed, blinking over and over, heart pounding. God fucking hated him. Why would he get this now, when he couldn't see? Couldn't travel? Couldn't have a life?

"Hey, you." Bax's voice came from right near the door. He knew the room well enough to know that. And damned if Bax didn't sound tickled about something.

"Hey." He smelled hamburger meat. "Momma making y'all supper?"

"Coke's cooking. Momma went out with Jack. I figured she needed a night out."

He could hear the thump-scrape of Bax moving closer before the bed dipped, Bax reaching over to touch his knee.

"How's the leg?" His own leg moved, without him even thinking, pushing toward that touch.

"Aching. You know how that goes. Has to hurt to heal." Before he even knew it, Bax was leaning on him, touching him all along one side, that hand sliding up...

"Uh-huh." He turned toward that heat, spreading his legs more. Hey. Hey, Bax.

That hand flattened right over his crotch, resting there as if it was meant to, and Bax smiled against his cheek. "Good nap?"

"Yeah. Yeah, real good. You?" Shit, he was just vibrating with the sheer joy of touching, being touched, the whole damn thing.

"Uh-huh. Slept good for at least an hour. First time since our shit hit the fan." Bax rubbed him a little, back and forth, almost as if it was meditative or something.

"Good." He took a deep breath, shifting, sort of focused on that touch.

"Mmm. This okay, Jase?" Listen to that man. He could hear the roughness in Bax's voice, hear the fucking rasp of those calluses against him.

"Yeah. Better than."

Bax had the most beautiful hands.

"I was hoping it would be." Those lips edged over to his, Bax kissing him long and slow. Just like in his dream that wasn't a dream.

He couldn't fucking believe this. None of it. Not since he'd woken up in the hospital and...

Oh.

He stroked Bax's jaw, exploring, not willing to waste his time on the bad.

Bax licked at his lower lip, then pulled away a little. "We got to talk, Mini. But this is all right now. Yeah? Just for now?"

"Yeah. Yeah, Bax. I just. Let us have this." He'd do the hard parts later.

"Oh, thank God." Pressing him back, Bax pushed up against his side, that cast making a ridiculous noise against the edge of the bed. Poor Bax. The man was clumsy as Hell at the best of times.

He chuckled and pushed closer, hand on Bax's ass. "You're something, buddy. I swear."

"Just promise me you won't run screaming when you find out what." Laughing, Bax crowded him, hand working him like there was no tomorrow.

"I won't run. Hell, I'd smack into something."

That had Bax laughing harder, the sound truly happy, making him blink even though he couldn't see. Then Bax was on him, kissing him breathless, just like they'd been doing this for years. Oh. Oh, fuck. He pushed closer, humping that hand as if he was a teenager, as if he had an itch that needed scratching.

"Mmm." They broke for air, then dove in again, and Bax finally worked that hand into his still-open jeans, closed it around his prick.

He made a strangled cry, the sound caught in Bax's mouth. Oh. Oh, God. No fair. No fair to take his life and give him the one thing he couldn't have…

Stroking hard, Bax gave him just what he needed, what he'd fucking wanted for years. That hard thumb rubbed up the underside of his cock, pressing just below the head, making him arch and thrash.

It was like a good ride, all motion and want and spinning. He tried to warn Bax, tried to let Andy know he was gonna be way quick off the mark, but it wasn't happening. And it didn't seem to matter one bit. Bax was pushing him on, making these amazing noises, just as hot for him as the Fourth of July.

Jason couldn't help it, so he went with it, giving it right up and crying out his pleasure in Bax's mouth.

"Jase. Oh, Jesus, you… Yeah. That's it. That's it." The touches slowed but they didn't stop, making him shiver with it. Almost too much.

"Good to me." He groaned, gasping with each little aftershock, each one seeming so Goddamn big.

"Shit, Jase. I been wanting to be this good to you for years." He got another kiss, slow and deep and almost like a fucking drug.

Yeah. Yeah, he knew that. The same things he'd wanted to do for Bax.

"Y'all about done? Because the burgers are ready!" Coke

shouted from the hallway, making them both jump.

Jason blinked, took a breath. "Yeah. Yeah, smells good, Coke." He leaned into Bax a little. "Shit. I forgot all about everything."

"Me, too." Stroking his back, Bax laughed. "'Least your momma wasn't here. Come on, Mini. Let's get cleaned up and eat. Coke wants to powwow."

"Powwow? What about?" That hand felt damn good, solid.

"Oh, no. I'm letting him talk. Come on, now." Bax shifted, levering up.

Hell, he could almost see the frown when that leg didn't cooperate.

"Okay. Okay, Bax." He got his hand on Bax's ass, steadying the man. Shit, he was feeling loose in his skin.

"Oh..." Bax slid and pressed against him a moment, then was up. "Get over here. This damned crutch ain't cuttin' it."

"Bossy old man." He stood, got himself all zipped and tucked, hands smoothing down the front of his shirt. "Am I okay?"

"You're fine." One finger flicked at his collar, brushing his neck. "I'm a little rumpled."

"I..." Fuck, he wanted to see Bax. Right now.

Needed to.

Bax turned, giving him a hard, quick hug. "It'll be all right, Mini. I know it."

He didn't know about that, not at all. Still, it was better right now than it had been this morning, so he'd take it.

For now.

Chapter Seventeen

Bax sat, wiping his hands on his cut-offs before nodding to Coke. "Smells good, man. Thanks for making supper."

Coke nodded at him, dark head bobbing. "Welcome. It ain't fancy, but it's food. C'mon, Jase. There's a plate for you."

"I ain't hungry." Jason stayed at the doorway and Bax could hear Mini's stomach trying to eat itself.

"Bullshit. It's chips and burgers. There ain't nobody here but us. Andy knows how you like 'em."

"Yep. And I promise I won't cut it up like Momma did." He'd seen how Brenda fixed Jason's plate. Lord. "Come on, Mini."

"Okay." Jason stepped forward, slow and careful, making it to the edge of the counter before stopping. "Help me out?"

"You know it." Before Coke could move, Bax was up and there, hand on Jason's arm. "Come around to the left, now reach out and feel the seat."

"Thanks." Jason relaxed, nodded. They needed to get him out of here, into a place where he felt like he could figure this shit out.

Jason got settled and Coke put a plate in front of him. "The burger's in the front close to you, then the chips are behind it, 'kay?"

Bax vaguely remembered some after school movie where a blind guy did his food on the plate by the clock or something. Maybe they'd try that. Later. "Lessee, you want lettuce, tomato, mustard and a tiny bit of onion, right?'

"Yeah. Yeah, thanks." Jason's fingers slid around the edge of the plate, exploring, and Bax and Coke shared a long, sad look.

Then Coke's lips went tight and those dark gray eyes just flashed. "You want a Coke, Jase?"

"I'll take a beer, man."

Well, a beer was better than a whiskey. They'd go from there, since Jason was willing to eat. "One. Then you switch to Coke."

"Bossy." Jason's eyes landed on him, just staring, and shit that was weird. "I'm a grown man, Bax. Don't."

"Stop it. We'll all have a round and then switch. There's not but a six pack left." Coke to the rescue.

Bax sighed, rolling his shoulders. "I'm not trying to be the boss of you, Jase. We need to talk, though. We'll all need a clear head for this, okay?"

"Okay. Okay, man." Jason frowned, grabbing a chip. "What's up? I mean, beyond the obvious, gee, you're fucked part."

"Well..." He took a deep breath, appealing to Coke with his eyes. "We got this plan..."

"Yep." Coke nodded, sat. "You ain't gonna get better with your eyes, are you, Jase?"

"Damn it, Bax. Do you have to tell everything?"

"I didn't tell Momma!" He wasn't no tattler. "Goddamn it, this is Coke!"

Jason snorted and Coke chuckled. "Y'all know that I'll nag till I know. Besides, it doesn't matter. The fact is you can't see, right?"

Jason clenched his fists around the edge of the plate. "Yeah."

"Okay, then. We got to figure out how to get you back up on the bulls."

"That's not funny, Coke." That plate jittered on the table, trying to crack.

Now it was out, Bax knew he had to throw in for Jase to believe it. "It ain't meant to be, Mini. You could do it with your eyes closed, you always said. Didn't you prove it on a dare? The only thing you need us to do is get you in the chute, and get you out of the arena."

"They ain't gonna let me ride like this. Nobody's gonna let me ride like this."

"Nobody's going to know, Jase. Nobody but a couple of us." Coke slid the plate out of Jason's hands.

"He's right. We'll get a couple folks, get AJ to let us use his place." Nibbling at a chip, Bax stared at Jason, reading that body language.

"I... Y'all are out of your minds." Jason looked a little panicky, a little shocky.

"I told Coke the same thing. He convinced me." Shit on it. He reached out and grabbed Jason's hand, rubbing his thumb in circles. "You can do it, Jase. You're the best rider there's ever been."

"I cain't see, Bax. People are gonna notice. The guys will notice. The press. I cain't see."

"Your eyes still track." It kinda creeped him out, but they did. "If we're careful, they won't notice. We could have you on a machine by the end of the week."

"I haven't even figured out how to shave, yet."

"So, we're not asking you to go to the finals this year, Jase." Coke still sounded so logical. "Train till next season, do some Venture events to keep your status then. You can learn to do this."

Bax held that hand, squeezing hard. "We got time. Plenty."

"This is crazy." Jason squeezed back. "Y'all are crazy."

"Well, no shit. Look what we do for a living, Jase." Coke rolled his eyes.

"He's rolling his eyes at you, Jase. You gonna let him get away with that?" He wasn't sure whether to bust out laughing or just cry. "We can start on the barrel, just to see what you think."

"You're serious, Andy?" Jason faced him, ignoring Coke altogether. "I don't want to look like no fool."

He reached up, tracing the lines etched next to Jason's mouth. "I wouldn't do this to you for nothin', Mini. I think it's crazy as Hell, but it's so crazy it could work. You ride with your body, not your eyes."

Coke cleared his throat, stood. "I'm going to take a shower, boys. Y'all talk on it, eat." Coke met his eyes, the look knowing, sure.

"Thanks, Coke." Nodding, Bax watched Coke go, then turned back to Jason. "You can do it."

"Bax, I don't know. Shit, I… I gotta sit down to pee, still. You're talking about traveling, hotels, different arenas, all that noise."

"No. I'm talking about going to AJ's ranch, where we can work for a year. We can start small, work up. And I'm right here." Goddamn, he needed Jason to believe. In himself, in Coke. In Bax. *Something*.

"I… You talked to AJ already?"

"No. Coke made some calls. Nate's in. AJ's supposed to call back when his wife gets a hold of him. She doesn't know." AJ wasn't the be-all-end-all, though. They could get someone with a ranch.

"Nate, too? I… You think the sponsors'll keep me?" Oh. Oh, hell yes. That was interest there.

"They never have to know. If it goes bad they'll drop you. You tell them now, though, they drop you anyway." That was a Hell of a hook. He knew it was. Go him.

"I… You really think I could? You… You'd stand with me?"

"I'll pull your rope, schlep your gear and tell you what you're seeing. I'm with you." He didn't know what else to say. He loved Jason beyond reason. But above all that, he believed Jason could win a title without seeing a bit.

"I… I'd try. I think. Yeah. Yeah, I'll try." Jason reached for his burger, fingers shaking.

"Then you'll do it." He moved the plate surreptitiously, putting it back where it had been, right where Jason needed it to be.

"I think so?" Shit, he hated that timidity.

"Mini. Eat your burger. You're always a mess on an empty

stomach. And Momma made lemon meringue." Jason loved tart with his sweet.

"Oh, man. I do like that." Jason found the burger, relaxed a little more. "This is hard, buddy. I thought about lots of things, lots of ways to get hurt, but never this."

"I hear you." Hell, it had never occurred to him. He'd known guys who had to learn to walk and talk again. But damn. Bax dug into his own burger, chuckling at how well done it was. It did his heart good, to see Mini eat, to see Jason rest and just sort of be for a second. It was the first time that hard face had relaxed since the accident, and man, Bax reveled in it. Coke came in, smelling like Old Spice, and Bax grinned at him.

"You gonna eat with us, old man? We're a go."

"You know it." Coke clapped Jason on the shoulder, grinning ear to ear. "That's the Jason I know. Brave fucker."

"Yes, sir." He handed Jason a napkin, tapping his free hand with it. "Right side. Mustard."

"Thanks." Jason wiped his mouth, the whiskers there heavier than he'd ever seen. "Y'all are going to get tired of helping me."

"Bullshit." Coke didn't even hesitate.

"No way. I tell you what, Mini. I'm gonna clock you, you don't stop putting yourself down." No one put Jason down. No one.

"Fuck off. You don't think I have reason? I don't know how to do this!"

"I know! Shit, you think I don't know? I want to know what to do to make it all go away, but I cain't!" Goddamn it, they had to start thinking positive, though, right?

"If you two are gonna brawl, go outside. Missus Scott don't need her kitchen busted up."

"Oh, you hush." That had him grinning, though, shaking his head. "All right, Mini. I'll calm down. I just... You're. You want some pie?"

"No." He damn near growled when he saw Jason's grin. "I want another burger, if there is one."

Coke was up and over at the stove before he could blink, dishing up another burger. "You want pickles?" Coke asked. Yeah, Jase liked the sour stuff on the side.

"Yeah. On the side. Please."

Well, he'd be damned.

Maybe this would work out after all. Bax finished off his supper. Somehow the sick feeling in the pit of his stomach wasn't near as bad as it had been.

Chapter Eighteen

Jason sat in the bathtub, soaking.

He could hear Momma pottering, could hear the TV in the guest room going, Coke laughing at something. Bax'd bathed and headed to bed and he was just sitting.

Thinking.

He couldn't fucking believe they wanted him to get on a bull. To lie to all those people. He couldn't fucking believe he was thinking about giving it a shot. Jason searched for the soap, chuckling at himself. Jesus, he'd done it once, though, on a dare.

Got up on that fucking bull, rode, easy as you please. Won a thousand dollars off Harry White, too. Smart-assed bastard.

A knock sounded at the door, not Momma. She'd never knock that hard. "Mini? You coming to bed?"

"Huh? Yeah. Yeah, I was just..." Rubbing a little with the soap, daydreaming, floating.

"Can I come in?" Lord, that whisper was loud enough to travel all over the house.

"Door's not locked."

Man, those hinges creaked.

He heard the thump-step-thump-step, then the clack of the toilet lid going down. "You okay?"

"I think so? I was soaking. Thinking about what all we'd said."

"I can go..." Bax sounded like he had a clog in his pipes. All froggy.

"I don't mind sitting and talking with you." He smoothed the soap over his thighs, pushing in a little.

"Oh. Okay. Good." Clearing his throat, Bax went on. "So you hear your momma and Jack come home? They were plumb tipsy."

"It's prob'ly good for them." He did like the smell of this soap, the way it felt as it slid.

"Uh-huh. They needed to blow off some steam…"

Lord, Bax was all stuffy or some such. Bless him. "You good, Bax?" He soaped up his belly, ass sliding a little on the tub.

"Huh? Oh. Sure." The cast clunked against something when Bax shifted, and Andy moaned, the sound low and rough.

He sat up, reaching out. "Bax?" No hurting his Bax, now.

"I'm okay. I just… Goddamn, Jason. You look… Fuck."

Well, now. That maybe wasn't pain.

"Huh? I… Oh." He blushed, hand dropping down to his cock, which didn't help, because his dick just went *sproing*.

"Sorry. I'm sorry." Bax was struggling to get up now, the toilet clunking, something banging against the sink cabinet.

"Wait. Wait, what's going on?" Why was Bax sorry? What was the deal? Jesus fuck.

"I shouldn't be sitting here staring at you when you can't see me, Jase. I… It ain't right. You don't need me droolin' on you when you're just taking a bath."

"If not you, then who would I need?"

"No one, I hope. I ain't waited this long to share." Yeah, now that was more like his Bax. All snarly and chest beating.

"Well, then, quit being weird and sit." He didn't mind, the idea of Bax watching.

Enjoying.

Wanting.

"Okay." *Clank.* Man, it was amazing how much he could see in his head, just by listening.

"Dork." He hunted the soap back down, found the washrag, working on getting himself lathered again.

"Well, this is new, Jase. I'm not sure what all to do sometimes."

"Yeah, I hear that." Everything was different now.

Fucking everything.

"Not to mention that I can't just get in there with you…" Bax ruffled his hair, the touch sweet, light.

"Now that is a shame. That's something I'd like to do."

"I'll get the cast off eventually. For now you just scrub on up." He could hear Bax settling, getting set, like the man was about to watch a movie or something.

It was a little weird, knowing that those eyes were on him, but he managed, washing his chest, his arms, soaping up the mass of curls above his cock.

"Oh. Damn. Jase." Poor Bax sounded like he was about to strangle.

"Uh-huh?" He got his fingers around his balls, rubbing and tugging, rolling a little. Showing off, making himself feel good.

"You… I swear. You're gonna kill me. Been wanting."

He would swear he could see Bax out of the corner of his eye. Just for half a second, and just a blur. But right there. Oh. Oh, Jesus. Please. "You got me, so long as you want me, Bax."

"Then you'll be around a good long while. You're just… Damn. Look at you."

"That's your job." He wasn't going to waste a bit of what little he had left.

"Right. Well, I got that down to a science after all these years. Touching I might not be so good at." Poor Bax. The guy had a complex or something.

"I don't know, Bax." He shifted, remembering those hands on his skin. "If you're not so good at it now, I'll go crazy once you're in practice. There ain't nothing like your hands."

One of those hands landed on his shoulder, squeezing, digging in to massage a little. "You think? It felt good, huh?"

"Better than anything." He let himself lean, let himself feel.

"Yeah. Yeah, I thought I might just die happy." Bax

laughed, the sound rueful as all Hell. "That was kind of a shitty thing to say, huh?"

"Nah. I mean, I wonder if it wouldn't've been better for everybody, if I had…" If he'd just never woke up.

Fingers digging into his shoulder, Bax made a rough noise. "No. No, it wouldn't. I need you, Mini. I'm selfish enough to say it."

"I just…" He bit his bottom lip hard. "What if you get tired of all this? I wouldn't blame you, not a bit." Bax deserved better than half-broke.

Shuffling, shifting, Bax bent, lips on his all of a sudden. "Not gonna happen. Shit, if I didn't when you were a cocky shithead, I sure won't now."

"I'm still a shithead." He took another kiss, then another.

"You are," Bax murmured into his mouth. "You about done?"

"With the bath, yeah." The rest? He wasn't near done with that.

"Uh-huh. I'm slipping here, Jase." Huffing a little, Bax let go of him and stood. Those hands were right back, though, tugging at him, helping him rinse.

He dried himself off, and got Bax moving down the hall before those hands made it impossible to move, to walk right.

It wasn't easy as it was. Bax leaned on him, using him as a crutch, and that meant those clever hands were all over him. All. Over.

"Bax. Bax, you're gonna make me all…"

Yeah.

Hard.

"Uh-huh. I hear that. You think it's easy with the cast and shit? Whoa, Mini. Turn." Bax teetered, but they made it through the bedroom door.

Jason actually laughed, tickled by them, by the way they were almost running a three-legged race.

"Shit, Mini, don't make me laugh. I might fall." But Bax was chuckling, the sound merry and relaxed, easing him

103

deep down.

"No falling for you, man. Get your ass up on the bed."
Fine bastard.

"Help me get out of these damned cut-offs, will you? That
was one reason I couldn't sleep." Yeah, Bax had come out
of his own bath bitching that he needed more clothes. Some
sweats or something.

"Well, if you weren't so tall..." He found Bax's fly, worked
the zipper down without catching that pretty cock.

"I ain't that tall. You're just unnaturally tiny." They both
tugged and Bax wiggled and it turned into some kind of
torturous dance, all heat and grunt.

"I ain't tiny, butthead." He leaned down, yanking harder
and damn near going ass over teakettle, cheek landing right
against that heavy shaft.

Oh.

Bax sucked in, that sweet cock sliding and twitching
against his face. "Christ, Jason. I. Damn."

"Uh-huh." He took a deep breath, sliding up along,
feeling. Smelling. Fuck.

Pushing up, Bax rubbed up on him, panting. "Feels like
nothing else, ever."

He moaned, headed south, lips finding the base where
cock met balls. Oh. Soft. Fuzzy. Shifting, restless, Bax
moved against him, hand on his head, fingers in his hair.
The scent of the man made him crazy.

His towel fell away and he let his mouth open, tongue
sliding over that hot skin. Oh. Oh, sweet Jesus. He could...
Yeah. Bax.

"Fuck, Jase. I can't. You're gonna make me crazy. Your
fucking mouth..." Poor Bax was just babbling.

He could handle crazy.

Jason didn't hurry—he was real caught up in exploring.
The big vein on Bax's cock throbbed against his tongue,
the ball sac shifted and wrinkled under his hands. Every
motion of his mouth had Bax shifting and sliding on the
sheets, the sound so crisp and real. That lean body felt

good. Right. Hot as Hell.

He got his lips around the tip of Bax's dick, started sucking, nice and easy, just drawing that salt and bitter flavor in. Bax started humping, short, sharp jerks of his hips pushing that flesh into his mouth. Jesus, someone was wanting so bad.

He'd not done this much and, when he had, it hadn't been like this. Hadn't been so goddamn fine. He could spend time, licking and sucking at Bax's cock.

"Jason..." Bax was petting him now, hands moving on his shoulders, tracing his muscles and bones, the touches hard and needy. A man could get addicted to that, too.

"Mmmhmm." He nodded, the tip of Bax's dick bumping against the back of his throat.

"Oh, Jesus fucking Christ!" Lord, Bax kept shouting like that he was gonna have Momma in here, or worse, Coke. Liquid heat slid down his throat in tiny drops, Bax so wet for him. Those soft balls were drawn up tight, so he got hold of them, rubbing and rolling as he swallowed hard, toes just clenching.

"Uhn!" That was it. Bax came for him, hard and fast, cock swelling impossibly in his mouth. Andy shook with it, a long, low groan falling down on him. He took what he could, heart hammering in his ribcage. Goddamn. He wasn't never going to have to wonder about that flavor. Not ever again.

"Jase... God." Moaning, Bax stroked his cheeks, thumbs rubbing just along his jaw. "You. Damn."

"Uh-huh." He nuzzled into Bax's belly, hand working his dick good and hard. So good, his Bax. His cowboy.

"I... Jase. C'mere. I want to help you out." Tugging at him, Bax moved him up where his face could settle against the hard curve of one shoulder, where one of Bax's hands could grope along his ass.

"Cowboy." He wanted so bad it ached, his balls rubbing against Bax's thigh.

"Yeah. Oh, God, yeah." Bax finally got him in one hand, the other still holding his butt. The feeling was like nothing he could describe, his cock pushing through Bax's lean fingers.

He gasped, eyes wide as he fought to see, fought to feel and breathe and...

Oh. Oh, fuck.

Bax gave him all the heat and pressure and friction a man could want, tugging at him, pulling up and down. And that other hand... Oh, God, it was just moving, touching him in places he'd never wanted anyone else to touch.

"Bax." His head snapped back and he shot, hips jerking violently.

"Jason." Bax whispered his name, sounding awed as all get out, those lips pressing to the side of his mouth.

"Yeah." He turned his head, taking a real kiss.

Bax gave that up to him, too, holding him close and kissing him hard. Full-on, no stopping, just like Bax did everything.

It wasn't all he wanted, but it was way more than he'd ever hoped for.

Chapter Nineteen

Bax woke up about as happy as a man with a broken leg could be.

Jason lay curled up along his side, the door was closed, and he had a lingering memory of Jason's mouth on his skin. That was like a fucking miracle. Of course, the best part was that Jason had said yes. He'd try to ride. That made Bax so happy he could bust. They'd have to get Coke to call AJ and see what they could set up.

Right now, though, he'd just wake up a little, let his fingers do the walking that his leg couldn't. All up and down Jason's back. Jason moaned soft and low, the sound familiar, something he'd heard in the dark of the night a hundred times.

"Shh. I got you, buddy." He wanted Jason to wake up, but he knew Mini needed his rest, too. Besides, these days, waking up was kind of a terror for Jason.

"Bax." Jason scooted closer, lips brushing his jaw. "I can see you when I'm sleeping."

"Yeah?" That was kinda sweet. "Like from before?"

"No. No, I don't think so. Your cast—it's blue?"

"Yeah. Yeah, it is." A chill ran down his spine. "How is that possible?"

"There ain't nothing wrong with my eyes, Bax. They see just fine. It's just that I cain't make sense of it in my brain at all."

"Oh…" Bax thought on that, then laughed a little. "So I can make faces at you today and you can see me tonight?"

"I might. I might not. There ain't no rhyme or reason to it, you know? 'Cause they're dreams." Jason shrugged, sighed

107

a little. "It's just like you, dreaming about something that happened in real life."

"Oh." Well, shit. Maybe that meant that Jason wouldn't see the absolute stupid expression he knew was on his face every time he looked at the man. "How you feeling?"

"Sorta fucked up, I guess. I mean, I never thought I'd get to...to know things about you like I do now. It ain't fair, to be able to love you and be all broke."

"Hush, now. You're not broke. Just bent in the brain area." Bax shut them both up after that by turning some and taking a nice, slow kiss. He was really going to have to remember how well that worked. Nothing shut Mini up that quick before, ever. They both moaned a little, and this time Jason was wide awake for him. Wide awake and right there, warm and good. Jason's eyes were wide open, moving all around, jittering some. That tongue, though, it was working his lips, pushing in and touching him, tasting him.

Bax closed his own eyes, not wanting to see Jason trying so hard to find him. It hurt, bone deep, and he knew it had to be Hell for Mini. The kiss took on a whole new layer when he sank into it like that, and Bax pushed at Jason, yelping when his leg protested.

"Easy. Easy, Bax." Jason frowned and reached for him, holding down his leg.

"Sorry. I got caught up in the ride." His eyes had popped open when he hurt, and that little frown on Mini's face made him want to laugh. Always worrying about him.

"You tend to do that. Good thing I'm good for more than eight seconds."

"You know it. You always are." That had him grinning like a fool, and wondering if Jason would see it in his dreams.

"Touch me, cowboy. I got a need." Jason brought his hand down, brought it to that hard, heated cock.

"Well, it would suck if you didn't, seeing as I'm all ready to touch..." His hand closed around Jason automatically, fingers squeezing down, thumb sliding along the length.

"Bax." Jason rippled, hips rocking as if he was wanting to ride.

"That's it, honey. That's just right." Oh, he loved that body, the way it centered, just flowed, every muscle designed to do just what it needed to.

Jase tucked his chin, entire body moving, riding his touch as that pretty dick slid over his palm. It was like watching the sexiest fucking bull ride ever. Bax approved. He kissed Jason's throat, his shoulder, licking the salt off that fine skin.

"Yeah. Yeah. Bax." The bed was creaking some, that flat belly going flushed.

"I got what you need, Mini. Just come on." Tightening his hold, Bax started pulling harder, needing to see Jason. It was as if he had to see, since Jason couldn't.

"Need you. Fuck." Jason's eyes went wide, huge, as heat poured over his fingers.

"Jason. Oh, Lord, you feel good." Hell, he was a selfish man. Bax knew that. He hadn't thought a bit about himself just then, though.

"Uh-huh. So good. Andy." Jason reached for him, tongue lapping at the corner of his mouth.

"You're fucking amazing, Mini." He slid his hand back, pushing to the base of his own cock, giving it a good yank. Hoo yeah.

"Uh-uh. Mine, huh? I waited a long, long time."

"Well, come on, then." He grabbed Jason's hand and brought it down, pushing against that callused palm.

Jason grinned, eyes rolling a little as those fingers explored him, sliding up and down along his shaft.

"Oh. Jesus fuck, Jase. I..." He couldn't hold back. All he could do was hump like crazy, needing to come like a freight train with no brakes.

"You're so fucking hot, Bax." The wonder in Jason's voice was right there, just all written out on the lean face.

"Nnnh." So much for coherent, but when Jason touched him that way he couldn't think. All he could do was shoot until his teeth rattled, a low, raw sound coming right out of him.

Then he got to see Jason bring that slick hand up, lick it clean. Jesus fuck.

His balls tried hard to empty again, his spent cock jerking. "Jason. You. I swear. I ain't never had nothing as fine as you."

"I... You sure, man? You sure you want this? I'm sorta as-is."

Bax stroked a bead of sweat off Jason's cheek, rubbing the sharp curve of one cheekbone with his thumb. "I got you. Been waiting on you. I don't care what condition I get you in."

Jason leaned in a bit. "Well, then. I reckon you can keep me."

"You'd best count on it, Mini. Not letting you go." No matter what Jason thought about how worthless he was now, Bax wasn't going to let go.

Ever.

Chapter Twenty

He wasn't ever going to get used to riding in a truck and not being able to see.

It just was too fucking weird.

"Where are we going, y'all?"

Coke's voice sounded right beside his ear and he could see the motion, the dark of Coke's cap, just out of the corner of his eye. "We're going for a ride down pasture, just so we can talk without your momma hearing, you know?"

Bax's chuckle came from the other side. "She's got a nose for news, that's for sure."

"She's a momma." She was fixin' to drive him crazy. "What all do we have to talk on? Coke, you're fixin' to have to go soon?"

"I got two weeks, still, maybe three. I got a hold of AJ. He's in, so's his woman."

"Coke says we'll have Nate, too. Maybe Dillon. We can talk on it. On who all you're comfortable with." They bumped off the track, Bax finally slowing to a stop.

"Where are we?" This was his fucking land. He shouldn't have to ask, Goddamn it.

"Just the pond, man. Come on." The air changed the minute Bax opened the door, which kinda freaked him out.

Jesus.

He closed his eyes tight, waiting for Coke to slide out before he headed for the passenger's door. He could feel the sun on his face, knew then, that the pond had to be in front of the truck.

"Come on, son." Coke's hand felt warm and heavy on his arm. It was funny, but he could feel the kindness through

111

Gramps' touch.

"I... Yeah. I'm coming." He wrapped his fingers around Coke's arm, surprised, sort of, at how thick it was. "You getting fat, Coke?"

"Shit. That's pure muscle, man." Coke flexed, snorted. "I got to play bull-tag." The muscles popped right up under his fingers, proving Coke right.

"Hey, no feeling up Coke," Bax said, sounding far away. It was fucking strange, how distance affected things when you couldn't see them.

"Man, I can't do nothing...don't drive the truck, don't feel up the bullfighter, don't yell at Momma."

"There's plenty you can do real well, Mini." Oh. Oh, Lord, listen to that man. That was Bax's bedroom voice.

He ducked his head, grinned. "Yeah, we'll see. Did y'all bring lawn chairs or are we walking?"

"We're walking, or hobbling in my case," Bax said before Coke could even draw a breath. "Just to get your feet under you. This is going to be a long process, Mini. We been talking."

"Yeah? Cause I been thinking, and I don't know how we can pull this off. I'm not that smart."

"Bullshit. You're a wily fucker, Jason. Possibly the smartest bastard out there since Ace Porter retired." Coke's voice got a little excited. "Oh. Ace. Ace could help..."

Bax laughed. "He sure could. He has an in with the management. The biggest thing is going to be the cameras."

"I don't know if I want Ace knowing." Ace was... Shit. Ace was everything any cowboy wanted to be.

"Sure, son. I can see that." Coke patted his hand, starting to lead him down the slope he knew led to the pond. "If he don't, though, and he finds out..."

Jason's boots slipped a little and it was hard not to panic, not to toss and jerk like a balky mule. "Fuck. I can't do this. I can't even walk!"

"Stop." Bax pulled him away from Coke, holding his arms, shaking him. "Did you ride the first calf you got on?

No. You got to work at it a little at a time, Mini."

"You try it. Shit, Bax. I gotta start all over at fucking everything!" Oh, it felt good to just holler.

"I know. I know, Jase. I'm fucking sorry for it, but I ain't sorry you're still here. 'Sides, I ain't walking no better. Could be it was me who made you slip." One thumb rubbed against his cheek, Bax touching him, letting him know someone was there.

He nodded, took a deep fucking breath to calm himself down. He could smell the water.

Really.

Weird.

Coke cleared his throat. "So. We'll have to go to AJ's, start there. Get you on the barrel."

"What are we going to tell Momma?" He could do a barrel blind. He could ride.

It was the rest that scared him.

"Well, I figure we'll tell her AJ's is more private. Or at least Coke will." Bax's chuckle had him smiling, too. Yeah, Momma was a lot more likely to believe Coke.

"AJ's got that little mother-in-law house deal, too. You and Bax can work on details without the whole world looking at you."

Sometimes he thought Coke was a fucking genius.

"Come on, Jase. Walk with us." Bax looped an arm through his, Coke holding the other side. They didn't pull him, though. They let him pick his way. It got easier, once they hit level ground. He trusted them not to let him go flying and he finally relaxed, wandered a bit.

"There you go." Coke sounded pleased as all get out.

It felt good, to stretch his legs, to be out in the sun again. Really good. Bax felt solid as a rock, even with the damned cast, which Bax was walking on more than he should. Coke was a little more gentle, but right there.

"We ought to swim," Bax finally said, sounding relaxed and happy.

"Y'all go ahead. I bet the water's great." There was no

way.

"Oh, no, son. Not without you." God, Coke could convince a priest to take his collar off. "We'll keep you afloat."

"Coke. I don't know." Fuck, he couldn't know where he was.

Bax squeezed his hand, fingers callused and firm. "The pond is just to our left. That big rock is almost right in front of you. We can put our clothes there."

He was going to fucking freak out like a buckle bunny at a meet and greet.

"Mini." Bax took his face between both hands, Coke fading away like a ghost off to his right. "Who do you trust? Who never lets you down?"

"That's prob'ly cheating, man." Still, he let Bax ease him down on the big rock, let Bax's hands slide down his arms. "This is tough, Bax. I keep trying to cowboy up."

"You're doing great, Jase. I'd be freaking out." His shirt got the same treatment, and if Coke wasn't there it would be kinda hot.

"I kinda am. I mean, we were just swimming a few months ago…" He wrangled his belt undone, got his jeans open.

"Yeah. It's—"

A low noise cut the rest off, Bax moving, the sound of cloth rustling seeming loud. He heard a whoop and a splash, and had to laugh. Looked like Coke liked to cannonball.

"That son of a bitch does know how to live."

"Sure he does. We should be so spry. Come on, Mini. Let's live a little." Strong fingers slid down his arm, palm pressed to his as Bax took his hand. "Slow and easy."

It was fucking different—the mud felt slicker, the water colder. The sounds were different here, bouncing off the pond and caught by the wind. He held on to Bax's hand, trusted that Bax wouldn't let him fall.

"Look at you," Coke said. "Way to go, boy." One big hand clapped him on the back, then he could feel the water slap his side as Coke took off swimming.

"I don't like this, Bax. Not one bit."

"You love to swim." Bax pulled him into the water, stopped them both out where it lapped at his chest. "I got you, Mini. I'm right here. Not gonna let go. Just float a minute, like you're just closing your eyes on a normal day."

Okay. Okay, he could do that. He'd done that. He closed his eyes, let himself relax. Float. Breathe.

"That's it." Moving right up to press against his ribs, Bax put one hand under his back, letting him rest there, keeping him steady. Hell, it wasn't like Bax could float.

It took a bit, to want to start moving, to actually do a little swimming. Sure enough, when he did, though, Bax was there. So was Coke. When he moved, they were like bats or something. Bouncing things back for him so he could tell where he was. They made it easier, made it feel like this was something he could handle. Something he could do.

"Looking good, Mini," Bax whispered when Coke struck off swimming again. That breath ghosted across his ear, making him shiver.

"Yeah? You like?" He couldn't help his grin, not at all.

"I do. You're glowing in the dark, though. Good to be out in the sun." Bax was still brown as a nut. He'd seen that in his dreams. All that brown against that bright blue...cast?

Shit.

"Bax? What about your leg? I mean, the water. Cast." That... Shit, he was addled.

"Well, I wrapped it up while you were staggering around with Coke." Poking him, Bax laughed. Andy had given up the crutches two days before, grunting and tossing them out the window.

"I wasn't staggering." Asshole.

"Oh. That musta been me." They floated around some more, and he'd bet Bax was feeling good being weightless for a while, too.

"This is good. Real good. Is it all nice and green still?"

"Yeah. I mean, it's getting a little brown around the edges, like it always does this time of year." Moving close again, Bax whispered low. "Coke's ass is blinding."

He hooted, damn near taking in water with it as he laughed good and hard.

"What are y'all cackling about that you're trying to drown Mini?" Coke floated over and Jason had this terrible image of his white butt shining like a beacon.

Man, he wondered if it drew the fish.

Him and Bax got to cackling, both of them just rolling with it, just like it used to be, easy and stupid and fine. The sound of water hitting Bax in the face made him laugh even harder. When Bax let him go to breathe, Coke was right there to hold on to him, making sure he didn't sink. It made him start to believe. Just a little.

Maybe more than a little.

At least enough to try.

Chapter Twenty-One

"Bax? Bax, honey? Y'all need to wake up. AJ's here to see you."

Jason's momma was knocking at the door, almost too lightly to hear, but it brought Bax up in bed like a shot. His rough movement almost shot Jason right out of bed. Damn.

"Coming, Momma," he called, settling his hand over Jason's mouth to keep the man quiet. "You just tell him I need to get dressed."

"I have coffee on. I'll tell him."

Shit. He lifted his hand as soon as he heard her walk away. "You okay, Mini?"

"I... I... Yeah? I guess. I was... AJ?"

"Yeah. Momma says he's here to see us." Hell, he wasn't sure Coke had even told Aje everything. "I'll go out first. Tell him you're in the bathroom. That way I can make sure he knows what's what."

"Jesus... Okay. Okay. I... Okay." Jason got up, headed for the pile of clothes Momma left out every evening, making sure everything was clean and matched.

"Stop." It was the easiest thing to grab Jason's shoulders, turn him around, and kiss him clean on the mouth. Of course, it would have been way more suave if he hadn't stumbled on the bad leg. Still, he reckoned Jason didn't care all that much about suave, then. Not the way the man responded to him.

Better. Much better. "I'll send Coke in, okay? I won't leave you hanging."

"I'm cool. I'll get dressed." Jason leaned a little bit, then straightened up.

117

He leaned in and kissed Jason's jaw, just underneath. "You're amazing, Mini. I'll be back, huh?" Bax pulled on some jeans and an undershirt before heading out.

"Well, well. Look at your lazy ass, finally getting out of bed. Good lord." AJ was standing there, grinning like an asshole, coffee in hand.

"Hey, I'm on hiatus." He clapped AJ on the shoulder. "Morning. You talk to Coke yet?"

"Yeah. Yeah, I been talking to him for a couple days. Had to drop some bulls off, figured y'all'd just fucking dither until the end of time." He got a shit-eating grin. "So I'm here to fetch y'all."

Oh. Thank God. He loved Momma and Jack, but Goddamn they needed to get a move on. Hell, he needed to start his own physical therapy, and Momma didn't have room for weights and shit.

"Well, that'll work."

AJ nodded, tilted his head. "So…he's really blind?"

"Yeah. Yeah, I am." Listen to Jason growl.

"Hey, Mini." Bax tried not to sigh, 'cause Jason would hear it and growl more. Instead he reached out and took one of Jason's hands, keeping it from starting to grope like he knew it would.

"Jase!" AJ's voice came out a little too loud, a little forced, but Bax could see the how tickled AJ was to see Jason up and moving.

"Hey, man. Who invited you?" Jason ducked his head, hiding behind the brim of the gimme cap.

"Coke, I guess. I needed to see you, though. Make sure you were among the living." AJ finally just brushed past him and gave Jason a big ole hug.

"Hey, buddy." Jason grinned, slapping AJ on the back. "You been good?"

"Austin James! What dragged you in?" Coke wandered in, hair still wet from the shower.

Lord. Momma's house was exploding with cowboys.

"Hey, Coke." AJ released Jason and pounded on Coke's

back, grinning like a fool. It helped Jason — Bax could feel the man relax.

"Lord, lord. Y'all want some breakfast? I got biscuits in the oven and sausage started." Momma kissed Jason's cheek and pushed a cup of coffee in his hand. "Mr. Coke, you want a cup of coffee?"

"Yes, ma'am. If it's not too much trouble."

Bax led Jason to the table with a hand under his arm, figuring no one would notice too much. Luckily, no one did, and Jason managed to get sat without having a fit, even if that jaw was hard as steel.

The noise in the house was just getting louder and louder — AJ hooting and Jack and Coke yammering. The TV news was on in the front room and the dogs were still barking at AJ's truck.

Jason was gonna blow a vein.

"AJ! Why don't you take Coke out and settle the dogs. Momma, I bet Jason would love some orange juice."

The TV clicked off, and Jack came to stand in the doorway, staring at him a minute before the old timer nodded. "Hey, AJ. You ought to come down and see that three year old I got."

"Yeah? I could do that, yessir. You coming, Coke?" AJ grabbed his hat.

"I'm gonna growl at them dogs, first, but yeah. Unless you need help, ma'am?"

"No, honey. I can cook breakfast. Y'all go."

Silence fell, all but for the sizzle of bacon and sausage and all, and Bax let out his breath. "Come on, Mini. Let's hit the head, huh?"

Jason's lips were set tight, one hand on his arm. "Okay."

He took Jason to the bathroom in the back, far away from everyone. "You want a shower?"

"Yeah. Yeah, I gotta get out of here, Bax. We gotta."

"We are. AJ's ready to take us back. I just know Momma will balk, so we need time to figure." He helped Jason get naked before he started the water going. Lord, he was all flustered and his mouth was still watering.

Jason stepped into the water, the steam starting up, all those lean muscles getting wet and slick. Goddamn. Swallowing hard, Bax sat on the toilet, staring at his hands. He just wasn't sure if Jason wanted him in there.

"Can you...with the cast?"

"Huh? Oh. Yeah. Let me get a baggie." Momma had taken to leaving him trash bags all over, bless her. Bax grabbed one and pulled off his cut-offs and shirt, wasting no time sliding right in there.

Jason grabbed hold of him, dragged him close. "Bax."

"I got you." God, when had he become the only solid thing in Jason's world? At any other time, Bax would have reveled in it. Now it just made him want to put Jason right again.

"No. I got you." Jason squeezed a little, proving his words.

"You do." That had him grinning, relaxing. Damn. "Hey, Mini. You feel good."

"I ain't feeling too bad at all." Jason settled him against that flat belly. "So what're we tellin' Momma?"

"I think we're gonna tell her that you need to just have a little time, and that AJ has that little guest house that we can rearrange without bothering nothin'." That would be a good start.

"That works. I just gotta get out for a while, even if I can't ride a bull."

"You'll have plenty of time to work on it. AJ's got the machine, all that training room." He stroked Jason's shoulders, letting the water smooth the way.

"Shit, I'm feeling like a new baby in some ways. I can't even figure out how to shave." Jason gave him a half-grin. "Course some shit I'm figuring out okay, huh?"

"You do real good by touch." In fact, Jason was doing pretty good at touch right then, hands slipping below the belt.

"Yeah. I have some incentive, huh?" Jason relaxed back, fingers weighing his balls, rolling them some.

120

His legs spread like a buckle bunny's in the back of a pick-up. "I... Oh. I guess so."

"You just guess?" Lord, something wicked'd gotten into Mini. Something wicked and fine.

"I think definitely." Bax went up on tiptoe on his good foot when Jason's fingers brushed the skin behind his balls, his whole body burning with the shock.

"That a good sound, Bax?" Jason touched him again, then one more time, that feeling liked to drive him wild.

His hands clenched on Jason's shoulders, his whole body rocking against that touch. "Jesus, Mini. Ain't... That... Christ."

"Uh-huh." Jason slipped down, mouth on his belly, free hand bracing him. "I got you."

"You do. Body and soul." Shit who knew he'd wax poetic when Jason touched him there.

"Mmmhmm." Those lips found his cock, wrapped around his dick and just gave it up for him. All the while, those Goddamn fingers kept tapping and stroking, scratching a little.

Squirming, Bax leaned as best he could on the shower wall, reaching up to grab the shower head, knowing it would give him better leverage to thrust. "Jason. Jesus."

That finger slid back, just for a second, as Jason took him deeper.

His eyes tried to roll back in his head, his hips snapping, and he nearly passed right out. His cock coulda drove nails. "Mini. Please."

Jason's eyes rolled a little and the suction got bigger, stronger. Then Jason touched him again, circled his hole and pushed in, just the littlest bit.

Bax stifled his shout by biting his lip, his head falling back as his cock pushed forward. He came like a ton of bricks, his body feeling as if he'd been on about ten eight-second rides. When his brain and body got all re-combobulated, Jason was panting, lips against his hip.

"You. What do you need, honey?" He wasn't sure if he

could move without falling, his leg throbbing, the rest of him limp as a dishrag.

"I'm good. I... Uh. Yeah." Jason went pink as could be, grinning against him.

"Yeah?" Well, Lord love a duck. "That was... Your momma's probably out there listening." That tickled him.

"Oh. Shut up." He got a quick, sharp bite on his belly.

"You're gonna have to help me out, Mini." There. See him give Jase a job. Up the confidence. Jesus, his knees were jelly.

"I got you. Just a second." Jason stood and turned the water off, then hunted the towels.

"Left about three inches, man."

There. Jason's hand went right to the towels, and Bax figured they were getting a handle on the directions shit, at least.

Jason got him pretty well dried off, eyes jumping around from one thing to another, every sound making them move. They'd have to do their research, see if there was anything to do on that. If not, Jase would just have to keep his head down. Shit knew Mini did that enough, avoiding the cameras right in his face.

Bax took a kiss, just a slow, lingering touch of lips. He wasn't gonna bring that up now.

"Come on. They'll be waiting. Momma'll be ready to bitch about eating or something."

"Yeah." They finagled their clothes back on, that soggy bag stuffed in the trash. Coke and AJ and Jack were back, sitting and talking quiet like.

Coke nodded to him, then to the kitchen. "There's food."

"Cool. You haven't eat us out of house and home yet, AJ?" Bax had to tease, had to just grab Aje and hug. "Good to see you."

"I ate your breakfast and Jason's. I let Coke go ahead and have biscuits, though. Jesus, haven't you had that cast on long enough?"

"Shut up." Bax whapped AJ's butt, then went to discover

122

them some food, grabbing the plates Momma handed over. He saw Coke casually ease Jason sat down, breathing a sigh of relief.

Both of them had sausage, bacon, egg and cheese biscuits, nothing that needed a fork. Orange juice because Jason hated hot drinks when folks were watching. Coffee with a lot of cream and sugar for him because Jack had made it. Bax settled in, smiling all around. "So you sold some calves, huh?"

AJ nodded, boots stretched out and crossed at the ankle. "I did. I got me some going to the Futurities, too. There's a good crop."

"Excellent. Jason and I were thinking we might go on back with you, clear out a bit and let Momma and Jack have some time." He winked at Jack for Momma's benefit, trying not to hold his breath.

"Well, sure. There's that mother-in-law out there that you can stay in. Missy loves company."

"No." Momma's voice cut across the front room. Damn it. "If you want to go, Andy, you go. Jason's staying home."

Oh, shit.

"Now, Brenda," Jack said, going to grab her hand. "I think it's a good idea."

"Have you lost your mind?" She looked just pure shocked. "Have y'all forgotten that he can't see?"

Jason started to stand, vibrating, and Coke grabbed one shoulder.

"Breathe, Jason."

"Momma!" Bax popped up like a jack in the box, reaching out to Jason. "That don't mean he's dead. AJ's got a good spread. Lots of space for us."

"There's space here. Jason knows it here. I'm here."

"I cain't just stay here, Momma." Jason bit the words out.

Sighing, Bax looked to Coke, who stood up and went to Brenda, putting an arm around her shoulders. "Come on and chat a minute, Brenda. Just hear me out."

Jack and Momma went with Coke into the kitchen, Jason

123

standing there, jaw clenched, AJ sitting with eyes big as saucers.

"Man, Jason. You look like you need a beer."

"No shit, AJ. I'd've never known if you hadn't said."

AJ grinned. "Well, I figured, you being fucking blind and all..."

"No beer. Not until we get to your place, AJ." Fuck, he just wanted to eat his breakfast.

Jason and AJ stayed still for a second, then the two assholes started to laugh.

His hands clenched into fists, his jaw setting hard. "You go on and laugh, you braying jackasses. I'll kick both your butts."

AJ snorted. "You need to fucking lighten up, man. Blind assholes know how to laugh, right, Jase?"

One of Jason's eyebrows went up. "I'll have to look in the Blind Asshole Manual, man."

"Yeah, but how will you read it?"

He was developing a tick. Right there, next to his eye. "I... I got to go outside. I'll be back."

AJ's backpack was right inside the door, and Bax rooted through it until he found a pack of smokes and a lighter, so he could head out to have one. Maybe three.

He got halfway through one before the screen door opened, Jason stepping out, heading right for the stairs. All he had to do was be quiet, let Mini walk right by.

Jason sniffed, head tilting. "You got one for me, Bax?"

Or maybe not.

"Yeah. Here." He handed one over and waited for Jason to figure out which end went in his mouth before lighting it.

"Thanks." Jason didn't say a word, just smoked, drawing deep, eyes closed.

Shit. Bax felt like a solid gold asshole. Jason was the one who needed some time, some kind of adjustment period.

"I'm sorry, man. I just got a little sideways."

"No sweat, Bax. I. You know you don't have to do this,

yeah?" Jason took another pull on the cigarette. "I won't drag your ass down, no matter what. I want you to know that, yeah?"

"I know that, Jase." His ass had been dragging for at least a year. Maybe more. He was getting old to play the game. "I want to do this, Jase. I just don't want to fuck anything up."

"Yeah, well, this is us, asshole. Fucking shit up is a special skill."

"Oh, fuck you." He laughed, though, coughing on the smoke he pulled in instead of pushing it out.

"Not here. We need a bigger bed and stuff."

"You know it." Wait. Wait, did that mean...? "Was that an offer?"

"Well..." Jason tilted his head a little like a puppy hearing a whistle. "No, Bax. You offered—I sorta accepted."

"Oh, God." He was hard as Chinese algebra, all of a sudden. "I want that."

"I never have, but it's you." Just like that made sense of it all.

"Well, yeah. I'd do the same for you." He so would, even if the thought made things down there kind of clench.

"Then we really need a good-sized bed, sturdy." Jason reached out, just barely brushed his hand. "'Cause you and me could ride, Bax."

"We could. We're good at that, too." He didn't know whether to shit or go blind. Okay, that was a bad analogy.

"Yeah. So, what? We pack some shit, but don't let no one see us pack my gear?"

"I'm thinking, yeah. We'll make it nice and easy." His brain was in his dick right now, but they'd figure it.

"Good." Jason scooted closer. "I can smell you, Bax."

"Yeah? I'm needing. Real bad." His zipper pressed hard against his cock, and he wanted to reach for Jason, do more than just touch his hand.

"I hear you." Jason leaned back, cigarette shaking a little bit. Bax knew it had to do with wanting, not fear.

He'd forgotten his own smoke, and it was damned good

he'd been reminded, because his butt was about to burn his hand. Bax stubbed it out on the planter by the steps. "Too damned many people."

"Yeah. I need to get out of here, get some space." Jason was rock-hard—he could see it, just waiting for him.

Bax wanted to touch. Lick. Suck. Anything. "Jason..." He was moving without even thinking on it, right up into Jason's space.

"Uh-huh. There's folks everywhere." Jason moaned, breathing in deeply.

"There's the barn." He wasn't above dragging Jason off. Even if they needed to go eat.

"There's my bedroom..."

"Hey guys, there any smokes left?"

He was going to kill AJ, and Bax couldn't quite bring himself to look at Aje until he cooled down, so he took another smoke for himself before handing them over.

"Your woman don't mind if we come?" Jason was fucking vibrating.

"Nah. Missy's ready. She's looking forward to having adults around who ain't me."

Yeah. Like AJ was an adult.

"She's a good one." Missy was weird as hell—earth-mothery and crunchy granola, but she put up with tons of cowboys and kids and dogs and the woman could cook like nobody's business.

Bax sighed, rubbing the back of his neck, the thought of all those kids deflating him some. "Well, we're gonna have to get packed and all. I guess we ought to eat. Has Jack calmed down the natives?"

"Coke's talking hard." AJ stared down at Jason. "You really gonna get up on a bull?"

Jason nodded. "I'm gonna try."

"Has Jason ever not done what he says he's gonna do?" Bax snorted, grinning finally.

"Well, not yet. Not yet. Man, you got balls." AJ nodded. "We'll make it happen."

126

"We will." They'd have to. No way was Bax letting Jason down. They'd make this work if it killed them.

"Well then, I guess I have to get some clothes in a bag." Jason stood up, AJ stepping out of the way.

Bax moved over, let Jason take his arm, just needing to touch a little. Something that no one would think on. "Some clothes, your new razor—"

"I'm not shaving yet, Bax."

"That don't mean you won't." He liked Jason with the stubble, but he wanted to help do the shaving, too.

"Yeah. Okay." They headed back and ran smack dab into Momma, who was all teary and red-faced and mad. "Jason. We need to talk."

"We do, Momma. I'm going. I need to. Period."

"But Jason, what do you think you're going to accomplish?" She was mad enough to use the big words, which always meant bad things.

"I'm going to work out how to piss standing up. I'm going to learn how to shave, how to eat, how to fucking function, Momma. I can't do that here."

"Why not? Who the hell taught you the first time?"

"Momma." Bax stepped in, frowning. "This is different. He doesn't need mothering. He needs a kick in the ass."

"He needs someone to take care of him, Bax. Until he gets back on his feet." She looked right into his eyes. "Bax. Please."

"I'll take care of him, Momma. I will. Hell, you know I'll call every other day." He did that anyway.

"Momma. I love you, God knows I do, but I have to go. I have to."

Jack appeared out of nowhere, weathered like the best pair of chaps, and he wrapped his gnarled roper's hand around Momma's arm. "Brenda. Honey, let the boys pack."

She backed up, her face screwing up a little when she started to cry again, but she nodded, arms crossing over her chest.

"I'm sorry, Momma." Jason sighed and headed down the

hallway, face more than a little hangdog.

Momma just watched him go, and Bax sighed, too, reaching out to hug her hard. "He loves you fierce, you know. He just don't want you to know how scairt he is."

"I know. I know, Andy. I'd ask you to promise to take care of him, but I know you will."

"I will." He kissed her sunburned cheek and smiled before nodding to Jack and Coke. "Y'all make another pot of coffee and I'll help him pack and then we'll all feel human."

"Okay. Okay, Andy. I love you, son." She hugged him tight, Jack shaking his head and watching them.

"You, too, Momma." Bax gave AJ a look when the man would have followed him, grumbling a little. He could do this by himself.

Jason was standing in the middle of his room, a shirt in his hand, looking just about gobsmacked.

"Mini?" He didn't want to startle, but he figured he needed to help. "What can I do?"

"Bax. I... I can't even pack myself. How...? How do people do this? How do people fucking live like this?" Shit.

"Well, they do, and they have for a lot of years, so I guess we can figure it." Closing the door, Bax went right over and wrapped his arms around Jason, squeezing.

Jason didn't say a word, just held on a second. "Come on. I need out of here."

"Okay. Your momma is making coffee. We should quick grab a cup, give her some kisses." Then they could hit the road.

"Okay." Jason nodded, walked toward the window, the path worn bare.

"Mini, come on. Help me pick out what you want. I know you hate that one scratchy shirt." That would help, at least. Jason could help pack by feel.

"I do. I want T-shirts and the boxer-briefs and Wranglers. Nothing white." Jase headed over, fingers sliding over the mattress.

"Okay. You want that blue shirt that looks so fine on

128

you?" Bax liked the dark green, too.

Those lean cheeks heated under the stubbly beard. "Yeah. Yeah, and the green. I'll need some sweats and stuff, too."

"Uh-huh. We need to buy some condoms." Maybe that was off subject, but he kept thinking about Jason and riding and inside. God.

"Okay. And slickery stuff." Jason nodded, strapping on his watch, fingers trailing over the little boxes of buckles in his top drawer.

"Yeah." Pulled over by that sad look, Bax put his arms around Jason again, kissing the back of his neck.

"Hey." Jason didn't whine, but those lips were so tight, Jason's entire body just vibrating.

"Hey. Who's got your back?"

"You do, just like always. Just like I got yours."

"You know it. I'm with you. We'll do it." Jason needed to hear it. Bax needed to say it.

"Okay, Bax. We will." That stubborn jaw set and Jason nodded, just like they were fixin' to ride.

He took a kiss because he couldn't not, spinning Jason the rest of the way to face him so he could mash his lips right down. Jesus. He needed to remember this — remember that his kisses were hot enough to melt Jase down and stop the damn fool from thinking. Not that he could think much himself, given that he was rubbing on the finest man in creation. They kissed hard, both of them pressing in, small sounds stifled between their lips.

Jason's hand landed on his back, palm flat, pushing them together. Bax moaned, his hips pushing forward, his cock trying to work its way free on its own. It couldn't, damn it, but it sure tried.

"Lock the door, Bax. We'll be quick, huh? Real quick."

"Uh. Shit, yes." He made sure Jase was steady on his feet before hightailing it to the door to lock it, unzipping his jeans on the way back. "Oh, damn, that feels good."

"Smells good. Bring it over here where it belongs, cowboy."

Bax went right over, shoving out of his shirt, struggling with his damned jeans over the cast, then reaching for Jason's clothes. He needed skin and air and nothing else between them.

Once Jase figured him out, the clothes went flying, Jason's hot little body smacking right into his arms. Skinny, hairy little man. Bax moaned, tilting Jason's head back to take a kiss, their dicks meeting and rubbing.

"Bax." Jason's hand was hard as a stone, landing on his neck and dragging him closer.

"More. We gotta—" His breath huffed out a moment, leaving him with an unattractive gurgle. "We gotta hurry."

"Uh-huh. Come on." He got another kiss, Jason's free hand wrapping around their cocks and rubbing but good.

His whole body arched, his head falling back a little, breaking the kiss. "Jesus, Mini. Gonna kill me."

"Uh-uh. Just gonna love on you."

"I know. Same here." His hands tingled, and he got one moving, pushing it between them to press around Jason's hand. Gave them a whole load of friction.

"Uhn." Jason went up on tiptoe, hips sawing back and forth, pushing and pushing, always driving.

It was like watching Jase ride a bull. Pure sex. God. He squeezed, Jason squeezed. Yeah.

"Gonna let you in me, Bax. Want that."

Oh, fuck yes. Whimpering, Bax moved faster, his hips sliding as if they didn't have arthritis, as if he was eighteen, as if he wasn't teetering on his bad leg. "Inside. Jason. Christ."

"Yeah. Yeah, Bax." Jason's lips traced his collarbone, teeth scraping, just a little.

He shivered hard, his balls drawing up. "Fuck, Mini. Do that again."

"Huh? This?" He got another little bite, his skin buzzing.

"Yes. Oh, God." He worked his hand faster and faster, his whole body shaking. Bax went up on tiptoe, trying to hold on long enough for Jase to be with him.

"Fuck." Jase bit, just a little harder, hips snapping, heat pouring over his fingers. Yes. Hell, yes.

"Jason…" Bax just lost it all over. His cock throbbed and his balls emptied and that was all she wrote.

Mini breathed on his chest, panting away. Goddamn.

"Better?" Bax sure was. He was boneless and happy and ready to take on the world again. Even if his leg was aching like fire.

"Uh-huh. Good." Jase nodded, humming a little.

"Okay. Okay, then. We should clean up and, uh, pack." Before someone knocked on the damned door.

"Right. Packing." Jason nodded, stroked his cock one more time. "Gotcha."

Shuddering, Bax moaned, so sensitive it hurt. It hurt good, though. Just the right way.

They could do this. They just needed to remember that they had each other.

Chapter Twenty-Two

Jason could see the map of Texas in his mind's eye. Momma was northwest of Dallas. AJ's spread was down near San Antone. That was damn near eight hours in a truck.

With Coke singing.

Loud.

He figured they had to be near Waco by now.

Had to be.

Coke'd gone through George Strait, two Alan Jackson, a Bellamy Brothers and this weird-as-fuck mix CD that Dillon must have given them. That boy was weird.

"Andy, AJ's wanting to stop, walk around a bit. You cool with that?"

Hell, he'd pay to get them out of Bax's truck and just let him sit in the quiet.

"Sure. Sure. You need to take a piss, man, or just stop at a picnic area?" Bax was sounding a wee bit strained, too.

Coke started muttering to AJ on the phone again and Jason turned to look back into the back seat where Bax was, damn near screaming when it didn't work.

"He's wanting some food, man, and to walk around. He says there's a Jack in the Box dealie right up the road."

"Sounds like a plan." Bax patted him on the shoulder, letting Jason know Andy understood.

"'Kay." He could hear the sounds of the road changing, hear as things slowed down. When they fucking stopped, the silence was just huge.

Bax cleared his throat. "I think I may be stuck in this position permanently."

"I'll just wait in here while y'all do your thing. Coke, man, can you dislodge Bax from the back seat?" There was no way he was leaving the fucking truck.

"Jase, you got to piss. I know you do." Coke was a stubborn cuss, patting his leg, clomp, clomp.

"I'm okay." What if the place was a one-holer? What if someone saw him? What if it was noisy?

"I'll go with Jase to the pot, you and AJ get us some food to bring back out here, huh?" Bax's voice sounded as determined as ever.

"No. No, I'm fine." He didn't have to. He wasn't going to be in a position to have Bax hold his dick so he could pee. Jesus fucking Christ, what was he thinking? Momma'd been right. He was a Goddamn fool.

"Go on, Coke. We'll be along."

The sound of the driver door opening and closing was loud as hell, the solid *whomp* reminding him of when Bax had won the option on that truck.

"Jason, you got to at some point. This is as good a time as any. Place is dead."

"This is fucked up, man. I didn't think about all the shit that I'd have to deal with. I didn't get it."

"Well, I figure if we thought on all of it at once, we woulda hid, huh?" The back door opened and closed, too, the big king cab echoing. Then Bax was opening his door, hand sliding under his elbow.

His body followed, just like it had a mind of its own, which Jason figured it sort of did but... Yeah. He'd been following Bax for years—why would he stop now? Bax got him going, nice and easy, murmuring to him. Hell, it was like Bax settling him on a bull. 'A little to the left'. 'Step up'. 'You got your sunglasses on...' He kept his head down, focused on Bax and that thud-slide, thud-slide of the cast on the floor. Three more weeks and it'd be gone, too.

"Okay, we're at the door." Bax stopped him, the feel of the air from inside rushing out at him, the smells of burgers and fries strong.

He could hear his heart slamming in his chest, the sounds of beeping and talking disorienting. Okay. Okay. He could do this. He could.

Damn it.

Bax kept on murmuring, the low sound of that familiar voice overriding everything. "Almost there, buddy. Here. Turn left."

"Okay. Left." He nodded, kept his head down, trusting in Bax's voice.

"Here we go." It was like suddenly being in a bubble again, the sounds out in the restaurant cut off when they stepped into the bathroom.

"Dude. Stinky." He tried to grin, tried not to look as if he was fucking freaking out.

"It's a men's room. Hell, AJ's guest room bath will probably smell worse. You know that's where he keeps his porn."

"Oh. Oh, man. Gross." He chuckled, stepped forward. "Okay, where's the urinal? Help me."

"You know it." Bax shifted him right where he needed to be, helping him so he didn't have to touch anything nasty.

"Okay. Okay." He took a deep breath. Jesus, this was hard. Harder than he'd ever imagined.

"Just pee, man. It's all good." Bax was trying to sound so reasonable, but he could feel the hand on his hip shaking.

He managed it, and the relief pissed him off—which, damn. That was funny.

"There." Helping him tuck and wash up, Bax sighed, leaning on him a minute.

"Thanks." He hated this. He fucking hated it.

"Shit, Mini. I'm just glad you came in. I got to do my thing now, okay?"

"Yeah. Sink's to the right?"

"Yep. It's one of them motion sensor ones." Bax moved away, the air just barely shifting. Sure. So all he had to do was wave, instead of fumble.

"Hell, you can't get them to work and you can see."

"No shit. You know I hate them things." Bax could damned near jump up and down in front of them and those sinks wouldn't come on.

That whole memory made him chuckle and he got cleaned up, feeling ten thousand times closer to human.

"Better, man?" Bax bumped him out of the way a few seconds later, the sink still running so Bax could wash his hands.

"Yeah. Yeah, I might live." They headed out, right back through the front door and into the fucking truck, this time with him in the back with Bax. It was tighter quarters, but better, Bax's good leg against him.

Bax patted his leg, got him settled good, humming along a little with the radio. "We got food?"

"Smells like it."

Coke's laugh echoed back. "I got them chicken finger dealies and fries and burgers, all."

"You're a gentleman and a scholar, Coke," Bax said, and Jason felt Andy lean over to get their stuff. Bax wrapped his hands around a drink cup.

"Thanks, man." He took a deep drink, then searched for the drink holder, got the cup in pretty easily.

Okay. Cool. Round one to the blind cowboy.

"Burger or nuggets first?" Everything smelled a little overwhelming, like grease and meat and grilled bread.

"Nuggets." He held out his hands, stuck his fingers in the gravy. "With gravy."

"There you go." Bax sounded like he was choking to death, trying not to laugh. Asshole.

"Butthead." He didn't try not to laugh—hell, he just busted out with it. Two broke and one bent cowboys in a Ford.

It could be a fucking country song.

"Hey, I could lick you off, but that would embarrass Coke," Bax said softly, fingers brushing against his.

Oh. His cock jerked, eyes going wide as he tried not to moan, sticking his fingers in his own mouth.

135

"Now, y'all know better than to get busy in my truck, right?" Coke asked, reasonable as you please.

"Ain't this Bax's truck, Coke, my friend?" He was not blushing. Not.

"Yeah, well... I'm driving." He could hear the smile in Coke's voice, could feel Bax's laughter against him.

They all got to laughing but good, and things seemed just fine, just like it ought to be.

Maybe they could do this thing. Hell, at least he figured out where the gravy was now.

Chapter Twenty-Three

Bax sighed and rolled his shoulders, his neck like frozen rope. Damn, it had been a hellacious trip, but they'd finally made it. AJ's place would be perfect for what they needed. The man was obsessive about his sport, and he had a wee indoor arena, even, along with an outside practice chute and all. A mechanical bull.

A pretty little guest house.

"Well, here we go, boys," Coke said, clapping him on the back as he helped Jase out of the truck.

Missy walked out of the main house, hair wild, baby on one shoulder. "Hey. You made it in time for the two a.m. feeding. Coke, honey, you're in the green room. Jase, Andy—I've got the guest house all made up. It's yours for as long as you need it. Now, where's my husband?"

"Right behind us, honey. He wanted to make sure the gate was done up." Coke went and gave baby and Missy a kiss.

Missy hugged Coke tightly and handed over the baby, who went like a charm. Then those arms were thrown around him, Missy kissing his cheek. "You're looking damn grumpy, Andy. You and me, we need to do some shots in a couple days, huh?"

"You know it. I been cooped up with these assholes for days." He softened that by patting Jason's butt where no one could see. Still, he could use a shot.

"And you." She grabbed Jason and squeezed. "You do find yourself some shit, man. No worries. You'll have whatever you need here, huh? I'll keep those fucking media vultures away with a shotgun if I have to."

Yeah, yeah she would, too. Some reporter came out once,

after it got out that little Benji was real sick and not likely to live. Missy came out with a sawed-off shotgun and blew the windshield out of their Honda.

AJ'd damn near busted his buttons with pride.

Mini nodded. "Thanks. Y'all are good folks."

"Yeah. We all are." Coke laughed as the baby burped. "Which one's this one?"

"That's Daisy."

"Well, hey, Daisy," Coke said, bouncing the wee one a bit. "I'm bushed. You think I can go sit with this one and just have some tea?"

"Sure you can, honey. If she fusses, there's a bottle on the breakfast table." Missy waved Coke toward the house, smiling as AJ pulled up. "Hey, baby. You need help with the bulls or you gonna wait to unload till morning?"

"I'll unload now. Missy show you the guest house, Andy?"

Bax nodded. "Yeah. You want me to...?"

"Nah." AJ's eyes were on his woman, just burning. Oh. Right. They were heading to the barn. "You take Mini and let him rest, huh?"

Then they were alone, everyone disappearing like smoke. Damn. Bax laughed a little. "You want a shower?"

"Fuck, yes. How's your leg and where's the suitcases and stuff and I'll carry."

"It itches." He'd all but forgotten his leg, but man it was stiff and sore. "Here. This one's yours." He put Jason's duffel right in those reaching hands.

"Thanks. You want me to lug yours?" Jason looked toward the lights at the big house, eyes fastened to them, even though Mini didn't know he was seeing them.

"Nope. I got my backpack. We'll get the rest tomorrow. Come on." He wanted hot water and a bed and Jase next to him without Mini's momma right there.

They made it down the driveway with the bare minimum of stumbling. He'd have to talk to AJ about stringing a light up so he could see a bit of something. The house had a light on, though, one over the front door, the place looking inviting as hell.

It was small, rustic, but damned fine, with a couch and a chair in the tiny front room, along with a one-wall kitchenette. The bed in the big bedroom wasn't skimpy, the bathroom full-sized, and Bax moaned at the sight of the tub. "We can have a nice shower, man."

"Cool." Mini was standing really still in the doorway, swallowing a little. "Okay, now. Help me out. What all's here?"

"Well, you want to start back at the front door?" That might be better than starting in the bedroom. "Come on. Drop the bag two feet to your left."

"Sure, let me take my boots off. My fucking feet are killing me."

"'Kay." He dropped the backpack and wished he'd kept his crutches, waiting for Jason to get settled. God, what a day.

"You want me to get your boot, man?" Mini's hat came off, landing on that duffel.

"Would you?" As if he was gonna say no to Jason bending over and pulling off his boot. Yeah. Right.

"Sure." Jason came right to him, sliding those callused hands along his sides and thighs as Mini knelt before him. Jesus fuck.

"Oh. Oh, Jase. Been needing to just touch." He stroked Jason's cheeks, staring down, feeling how sharp those cheekbones were.

Jason nodded, forehead resting on his lower belly, lips hovering near his buckle.

"Hot." Jason felt almost felt feverish, and Bax couldn't blame him. All day in the truck, moving, not being able to see.

"Tell me you locked the front door."

"I so did." No way was he taking a chance on Coke or AJ wandering in to mention something they forgot.

"Thank God." Mini popped his buckle, his fly. "If you

don't want, holler, but I… It's been a long damned day, Bax."

"I want. I want." He didn't want to take anything he shouldn't ought to, but if Jase wanted to give. Yeah. A long day.

"Me, too." His pants got to about halfway down his thighs, his tighty-whities dragged right along with. Then Jason leaned in, lips finding his cock, easy as pie.

Some things weren't hard to spot, even for a blind guy. Bax chuckled, his hips doing a slow roll. "Oh, God, Mini. Good."

Jason hummed, murmured something around his dick, tongue sliding on his skin.

So hot. He closed his eyes for a moment, letting himself feel it, letting Jason give. His leg wobbled a little, but held, and Bax groaned, feeling the touch of that mouth all the way down to his toes.

Jase wasn't in a bit of a hurry, eyes closed, lips and tongue just fucking exploring him, fingers working his balls, petting and stroking the insides of his thighs. Those lips felt fiery and soft, riding up and down his cock, and Bax's nuts drew up under Jason's touch, his belly like a board.

"Mmm." Those fingers slipped under his balls, tracing the skin just behind.

"Jason!" He went up on tiptoes, his cast creaking on his bad leg. *Goddamn. Yeah.* "More."

That mouth went down, fingers slid back and up and oh. Oh, fuck. That felt wild.

He didn't know whether to pull away or push back, so Bax just went with what felt good. He pushed back against Jason's fingers, then forward into that hot mouth. Mini stayed right with him, touching and sucking, loving on him, making him crazy as fuck. All he could do was hump and hum and ride it out, just like the best eight seconds ever.

Then that burning tongue scraped across the head of his dick, swirling a little on the way down, and Andy arched, rocking a little on the ball of his cast. Damn. His skin tingled, his fingers scraping over Jason's shoulders. His ass clenched tight and his balls tried to crawl up against his body, and... Yeah.

Oh, fuck yeah.

Jason took him down to the root, lips tight around the base of his cock, pulling good and hard.

Bax came, little fireworks going off behind his eyes, his belly tight as all get out. A shout burst out of him, the sound ringing through the little room. Jase eased back off him, smiling, looking about as peaceful as could be. Bax pulled Jason up and stumbled back to the bed, leaning a little. "Damn, Mini."

"Yeah. Yeah, Bax. That was fine." Jason rolled toward him, rubbing against him a little.

"More than fine." He wasn't no attention hog. Bax knew how to give back. He reached down and gave Jason a press through his jeans, squeezing hard.

He got a wild, wicked smile, Mini jonesing on him. "We could get naked, Bax. Keep that zipper from biting on me."

"We could. I like you naked." Bax sat back and pushed Jason up, working buttons and zippers and shit, trying to get to skin. Between them, they managed naked just fine and he propped himself on his elbow, staring down at the compact, fuzzy little body.

"You're something else, Mini." Bax started at the sharp curve of one shoulder, stroking down Jason's arm.

"Mmm. Your hands, Bax." Jase leaned toward him, stretching.

"All yours, buddy. I swear." His hands wasn't nothin' special. They were scarred and hard and rough, but he knew Jason liked 'em all right.

"Mmmhmm." Jason looked as if he was on cloud fucking nine.

Hell, Bax couldn't blame the man. It was pretty close to heaven. If only those pretty eyes could see. Didn't matter. Mini could sure feel him, feel him pulling and stroking. And he could sure as fuck watch for the both of them. Watch that pink tongue flicking out, over and over, to wet Jason's lips. Watch that wet-tipped cock push up through the circle of his thumb and forefinger.

"You... I... Damn, Jason." He didn't know what he wanted next. What he wanted to taste or touch. So Bax just kept on keeping on, kissing Jason hard, his thumb working the head of Mini's hot dick.

These harsh little sounds kept pouring into his lips, over and over, Jason giving it up for him.

"Fuck." Growling, he pushed Jase down, moving them around, and bent to suck the thick flesh right into his mouth.

Christ. Yes.

"Bax!" Mini sat halfway up, mouth open, throat working.

"Mmmhmm." Oh, yeah. Jason was leaking for him, hot as fire, and Bax licked hard, tongue rubbing up and down.

"You. You. Oh." Jason started rocking, humping up against his hand, into his mouth, looking debauched as all get out.

Him. He was doing this. His palm cupped those heavy balls, rolling them, pressing them up against the base of Jason's cock. His mouth went all the way down, his lips closing tight, and Bax swallowed. Needing. Jase came for him just like that, pouring into his lips, hips bucking like they were right out of the gate. Bax held on, keeping Jason from choking him, and rode out each spasm, humming to himself. Fuck, he loved that man.

"Goddamn." Jason flopped back onto the bed, laughing softly. "Oh. Better."

"Yeah? Good. I tell you, I thought I was gonna go crazy in that truck." Bax felt a little floppy himself.

"No shit." Jason gathered him up close, hand sliding up and down his back.

"Feels good, Mini." That was an understatement, but so true. "We could wait on a shower."

"Uh-huh. We could just stay right here a bit."

"We could. Get the blanket up on us." Snuggle. Who

cared about anything else? It was like, three a.m.

Jase got them settled, got one cheek on his shoulder. "I hope Momma will start to understand. It's gonna be better, doing it like this."

He wrapped his arms right around Jason, holding that skinny-assed body close. "She will. This will work, Jase. I promise."

"Shh." Jason kissed him, eyes closed. "We'll figure our shit out."

"You know it." Hell, a good night's sleep would go a long way toward getting them back on track.

Chapter Twenty-Four

doing the

He could hear knocking, rapping, tapping, but he didn't know where from. Jason sat up, hands out straight in front of him, trying to figure out where the fuck he was, what the fuck was up.

"Bax! Bax!" He stumbled up out of the bed, falling over something and slamming to the ground. "Andy Baxter!" Oh, fuck. Where was he?

"Right here, honey. Right here." Bax's hands landed on him, holding his upper arms, helping him orient himself. "Sorry, Mini. I was in the bathroom."

"Where...? What the fuck is that noise?" He held on, heart pounding. "Bax, Bax, I can't do this. I cain't. I can't wake up over and over forever and not fucking see where I am."

"Shh. Hush, now. It's just all new, is all. You didn't do this at your momma's once you got used to it." Bax stroked his cheek, solid and warm against him.

He took a deep breath, then another one, bound and determined not to lose it altogether and start screaming. The deep breath helped, so he took another, then another. "Hey. Hey, Bax. Sorry, I. I'd been dreaming."

"Yeah? Anything good?" Oh, asshole, laughing, stroking the back of his neck, tickling like crazy.

"Dreaming that people were hunting my ass, trying to get my hat." Stupid, but true.

"Oh, that's not a good dream at all." They got him stood up, Bax lifting him right to his feet. "You hungry? Or you want to hit the head and have a shower first?"

"I need a shower and stuff and I need you to show me around, huh?" He didn't know how to do this. Momma's

144

house he knew.

"You know it. Let me move the bags into the closet, huh? Then we'll do the tour." Bax sounded completely reasonable, which meant he'd at least gotten enough sleep.

"'Kay." That banging came again, rap rap rap. "What is that?"

"Huh? Oh, I dunno. I think Coke is helping roof something." That sounded about right. Coke would have been up hours ago.

"It's weird, hearing things and not knowing." He heard Bax put the bags away, heard the closet door shut.

"You'll get better at it, I know." Bax helped him up, helped him back to the bed. Shit, that was all Bax fucking did, for chrissake. "Let's start here, huh?"

"It's in the middle of the room, by a window."

"It is. The headboard butts up against the window, in fact." Bax led him around the bed, and he counted the steps. Two, three, five. "You go from here straight across to the bathroom."

"Cool. There's nothing in the way? His fingers found the edge of a dresser, followed it around.

"Nope. All you have to do is stay away from the wall. Looks like there was a rug, but they took it up." He could actually see that, in his mind's eye. The darker spot on the floor where the sun never hit.

Okay. Okay, he could do this. The bathroom was almost easy—sink, linen cabinet deal, tub, pot. He could do that. Hell, everything was just where he'd thought it was, and the water faucets were set up with the hot and cold where they should be.

He did his business—sitting down, which burned his ass—and washed his face, hands. "Okay. I'm ready for more."

"Yeah? How about a shower. You and me. Naked and all." Bax helped him turn to the shower, helped him find the shower head and angle it away.

"Oh, hell yeah. You got a bag for your cast?" The tub was

big enough, the water pressure strong enough to sting his skin.

"Yeah. I got one out of the backpack." Bax laughed, pinching his ass. "Wanted to be ready."

"Oh, man. I'm all about you being ready." He got his hands on Bax, exploring, touching. Oh, man. He did like the touching.

"You are. Well, here." Bax shoved one hand down below the waist, and someone was so ready.

"Oh." He bit his bottom lip, touching but good. "I want you."

"Good. It would suck if you didn't." Licking up his chin, Bax smiled against his mouth, reminding him how much he loved that smile, reminding him what it looked like.

His free hand went to Bax's face, fingers tracing the tiny short hairs at Bax's hairline, the laugh lines beside those pale eyes.

"Having a look, huh?" Bax kissed his palm, cheek rough as a cob.

"Yeah. Yeah, I thought it was bullshit, but... Yeah." He could see Bax in his head, clear as day.

"Cool. You're looking less droopy, man." Bax petted him, his chest, his belly, that hand finally wrapping around his hip.

"Feeling better. Feeling solid." The hand he had around Bax's cock wanted to move, so he started stroking, fingers sliding up and down.

"Oh, that's... Yeah." Bax pushed against him, rocking away, and he could feel muscles moving against his arm and chest.

His other hand headed down Bax's spine, hunting that fine, fine ass. He wanted a hold of that, wanted himself a handful.

Bax went still for a moment, then pushed back into his touch, moaning loud. "Jase."

"Right here, Bax. I got you." He did—he had that tight little backside, he had Bax's cock. He had just what he wanted.

"Got me." Bax nodded against his neck, kissing his collarbone. "I'm all yours, Mini."

Yeah. Yeah, he knew. Images went right through his mind—from his mouth around Bax's dick, to Bax inside him, to feeling Bax's ass all around him. He was gonna explode. Jason kept touching, kept his hand moving while his own cock leaked and throbbed, rubbing against Bax's leg.

"You needing too, huh?" Bax was a master at stating the obvious, but he got moving, got touching, grabbing Jason's dick.

"I been needing you for a long damn time." He went up on tiptoe, shivered a little.

"Tell me what you want, Mini." Bax pulled at him, palm against the underside, rocking him. That voice... Christ, Bax sounded like he'd swallowed gravel.

"I want... I want everything, you know?" He did. He might need it.

Bax nuzzled in, head coming to rest on Jason's shoulder as he nodded. "I know what you mean. I surely do."

"Good." He leaned and rubbed and rocked and just went to town. "We got time to play."

"We so do." Bax was leaning harder, now, pushing back, relaxing with every touch.

"You...you want my mouth, Bax?"

"Hmm? This is good." Lord, Bax was easy. He just liked it all. "What do you want, Mini? Want to go back to the bed?"

"We could do that." There were things they could do in the bed that they couldn't manage as easily in the bathroom. They got the water turned off, shook off the bulk of it.

"Come on, then. You take me."

Oh. Asshole. Still, he could do it if it meant getting horizontal. He grabbed a hold of the base of Bax's cock and headed toward the bedroom. There wasn't anything in the way, if he stayed away from the walls.

"Jesus, Jase." Bax followed close, cock jumping in his

hand.

"Uh-huh. I got a decent memory." He reached out with his hand, found the bedpost. "See?"

"You do. Thank God. It woulda sucked if you'd tripped." They both laughed at that, and Bax bumped him toward the mattress, pushing them down.

He let Bax get that cast settled, then he swarmed over Bax, straddling the thin hips as he leaned down for a kiss. The kiss took his breath away, Bax cupping a hand behind his head, fingers rubbing, massaging. Andy just humped up against him, cock hard as stone.

"Need." His balls ached with it, his dick leaking.

"Anything, Jase. Anything."

Oh. Oh, God, Bax couldn't mean...that. Could he?

"I... Can we...? I mean, fuck." Yeah. Actually, he did mean fuck.

Bax went still again, but for his chest, which rose and fell fast. That cock didn't go down either, did it? "Yeah. Yeah, Mini, we can fuck."

"Oh." His belly rippled, dick jerking hard-hard. "We... we got stuff?"

"I think we do." Bax's face felt fiery hot against his shoulder. "I-I got some at the last store when we stopped for food."

"Oh. Cool. Where? I'll get it and then you can... I can ride, huh?" His heart was beating so fast it hurt a little.

"It's in my backpack. We can do it however you want." Jesus, that had to be hard as hell for Bax to say, but it made him want to holler, it sounded so good.

"It'll be easy to ride, then if we don't...if it don't work for us, we can do something else."

"We can. I'll get it." He got a kiss, then cool air when Bax hauled himself up to rummage through the closet and the backpack.

His hand worked his cock, up and down, nice and slow as he did some imagining, thinking of how Bax's ass would look, him bent over.

Bax was back in no time, hand closing around his to stop it moving. "Slow down, Mini. Want this to last."

"Yeah. Yeah, I... I hear you." Shit, he wanted to do this more than just about anything.

Bax kissed him, mouth hard and bruising on his. Those hands felt like steel on his shoulders when Bax held him in place, kissing him over and over. Everything went white-hot and sharp, the kisses enough to set him clear on fire.

Bax shoved him down and crawled right on the bed, before pushing up against him and rubbing like crazy. Lord. He spread, bucking, begging for it with all he was. The sheets were soft on him, the bedsprings singing—so fucking right.

"Want you, Jase. Want you so bad." Breathless, needy as all get out, Bax bit down on his collarbone, licking to ease the sting.

"Yours. Please, Bax. I want to know." He maybe needed to.

"Okay. Okay, babe. We can do this." Chuckling, Bax kissed him again before shifting around, muscling him up and over so he straddled those thighs, careful of Bax's cast.

"What do you want me to do?" He got one thigh hooked around Bax's hip.

"I just need to get you ready, huh?" They both knew how this worked, didn't they? They just had to get going.

"Well, then. Touch me, cowboy. It'll be easier after the first time."

"The first... Oh, God." That moan told him how much Bax liked the idea of doing it more than once. Yeah. Those slick fingers finally touched him, right where he needed it, one slipping into his body.

Everything started to slow down a little, his body moving, riding that touch.

"Hot. Oh, Jason, you're fucking hot." Bax's finger went all the way in, the feeling tight and hot, scraping.

"Bax."

That finger curled, and he cried out, lightning shooting

up his spine. "Oh! Again!"

"Right there, huh?" Bax was panting, voice sounding raw, and that finger hit the spot over and over, making them both moan.

"Uhn. Uh-huh. Uh-huh. Bax. Bax, please." He sat up a little more, shaking with it, it felt so good.

"Shh. I got you, babe. I got you." Two fingers stretched him almost too damned wide, the feeling huge, but sweet.

Jason pulled up on his knees, pushing up and out, spreading himself for his cowboy.

"Oh... Jason." Bax touched him carefully, loving on him, opening him up like no one ever had.

He'd never felt like this, never thought he could, and he wasn't going to miss a second of it. When he thought he might explode if Bax didn't get on with it, those fingers slipped out of him, and he heard the crinkle of a condom wrapper. "You ready, Mini?"

"Yeah. Yeah, cowboy. I'm fixin' to pop."

"Me too." The hair on Bax's thighs brushed the inside of his legs, and he could feel the head of Bax's cock poking at him, pressing against him.

Jason took a deep breath, pushed back and did his dead-level best not to get all tensed up. This was his Bax—the man would do right by him.

"I got you, Jase. I swear." One hand stroked his belly, his cock, keeping him revved up, ready to go.

"All yours, Bax. Show me now. I need to know."

"Mine." Sliding up, Bax slipped into him, a bare inch at a time. He felt fucking huge.

He gulped in one breath after another, toes curling, body not knowing whether to run screaming or just bust from feeling.

"Shh. Shh." One hand stayed on his hip, the other came up to cup his cheek, thumb stroking gentle-like. "Breathe, Mini. Come on. You gotta relax."

Jason turned his head, took Bax's thumb in his lips and sucked, nice and easy. Yeah. Relax. He could do that. He could.

"Christ. Gonna be the death of me." Bax laughed, breathless as hell, before starting to move, slow and steady.

"Mmm." That felt like nothing ever — Bax touching him inside, cock sliding and stretching him. So good. He knew Bax was staring right at him, could feel it like a touch. He could hear it in the way Bax moaned for him.

"'S good." He found a smile, found himself pushing back against every thrust.

"You know it is." Bax was humping, hips smacking his butt, starting to move faster and faster.

He wrapped one hand around his own dick, pulling good and hard, in time with Bax's thrusts.

Groaning, Bax moved faster, hands moving over him, touching his chest. Hell, Bax even pinched the hell out of his nipples, really letting him feel it.

"Damn. Damn, cowboy." His shoulders rolled, head slamming back, bottom lip stinging from his teeth.

"Kiss me, Mini." After bending him near double, Bax tugged down and leaned up and took a kiss, mashing his lips against his teeth.

His eyes flew open and he tried to see, so hard, with everything he was. It didn't work for shit, but it didn't matter. He could hear their skin slapping. He could smell Bax, hot and salty against him. He could feel that thick cock inside him. His balls drew up, almost aching, dick throbbing in his fist.

"M'close, Jase. Want to last for you…" Hoarse and raw, Bax's voice was another kind of touch, like its own caress.

"Gonna. Gonna. I." He arched, toes curling tight. "Oh, fuck."

"Jason!" Bax bucked like a short go bull, pushing so deep he couldn't tell where Bax started and he ended.

He shot hard enough his teeth rattled, his balls feeling like they'd crawl up into his body, then he slumped down.

Bax panted for him, groaning a little in his ear. "Damn. Hello and good morning."

"Uh. Uh-huh." He squeezed a little and they both moaned.

"Jase. God, Coke had to have heard that, even over all that banging."

"Mmmhmm." He gave Bax a grin, feeling settled in his bones, feeling wild and happy as shit.

"Slut." He could hear the laughter in Bax's voice, the admiration. Then the air went still and Bax kissed him hard. "Good, Mini. Real good."

"Uh-huh. Is it pretty outside, man?" He thought he could feel the sunshine.

"It is. You want to get that shower and go hang outside awhile?" Bax stroked his cheek, fingers gentle as could be.

"Yeah. Yeah, I do." He pressed into the touch, relaxing bone deep.

"Cool. Me, too." Kissing him hard, Bax pushed him up, kind of like he was a rag doll. "Take me to the bathroom."

"I. Okay." He took his first few steps, bowlegged as fuck, then he counted. Bed. Dresser. Closet. Door. Bathroom. *Score!*

"Damn, Jase. Good deal." Little things. He had to remember not to get growly when Bax got just as excited as he did about the little things.

"Yep. You didn't fuck my brains out." He was gonna get swatted.

"I tried awful hard. We'll have to work on it." The water started up again, the steam coming out right away, slapping his bare skin.

"Sounds like a plan." He searched the walls, looking for where the soap was, the shampoo. The nozzle.

"What do you want, Mini?" Bax stood back, letting him find his way, but right there if he needed the man.

"Just looking. Is there a soap dish?"

"Over in the middle of the back wall, just above knee level. Looks like Irish Spring."

Good old AJ and the manly soap.

"Least Missy didn't put in something bubblegum smelling." He got his hand around the smooth, sorta curved bar, grinning a little. He could damn near see it in his head.

"I would worry more about the kids putting liquid heat in the shampoo…" Bax drawled it out, laughing a little, the familiar rustle of a trash bag coming before Andy stepped in with him.

He chuckled, reached for Bax and started washing the fine asshole, being careful of that casted leg. This he could do.

"Mmm. Oh, Jase. You got good hands, buddy."

Listen to that man. Oh, yeah. That he could do. He nodded and focused, feeling each little inch of Bax's skin that he could reach. Jesus, it was fucking fascinating. Bax groaned and shivered for him, hands coming up to grip his arms. Maybe the sun outside was overrated.

Damn, this was a good fucking way to spend a morning. Bax seemed to agree, kissing him under the spray, their bodies moving together. That damned cast needed to come off.

He pushed up, hands cupping Bax's ass while the kiss went hard. That tongue pressed into his mouth, tasting him deep, Bax moaning for him. The sound went all the way to his toes. Man, that felt good. He took his time, just reveling in the whole all-by-themselves-behind-locked-doors thing.

"Mini…" Those soapy hands found his ass, squeezing a little, making him shiver. That was… Well, it was hot and uncomfortable, all at once.

"Yeah, Bax." He nodded, pushed back into the kisses, letting his hips shift like he was riding.

"I tell you what, Mini. You're hot as the Fourth of July." Bax kissed him again and again, licking his shoulder.

"You know it." He leaned down, rubbing his chin with its heavy beard on Bax's shoulder.

"Oh, honey. We need to shave you. You're scratchy as hell." Bax stroked his cheek, pushing his whiskers back and forth.

"I can't figure how." He pushed into the touch, humming low.

"I can do it."

Oh, now. That had possibilities. Jason nodded, moaned a little. Yeah. Yeah, that might work.

"Yeah? We can do it tomorrow." Bax bit on his neck some, rocking against him.

"Uh. Uh-huh." Damn. He was getting it up again. The water beat down on them, made them both slick and hot. Bax's hands felt so damned good. So hot. Damn.

"I'm likin' this place of our own thing."

"I am, too. It's damned happy making." He could see that smile in his head, the one he heard in Bax's voice. He got his hand around Bax's prick, not really jacking it, just feeling it.

"Mmm. Jase." They weren't neither of them in any hurry. Bax was mostly hard for him, hot, sweet in his hand.

"Yeah. I just want to touch a little."

"Touching is good, Mini. Real good." Bax shifted against him, slid against his hand, starting to get wet, and not just from the shower.

His thumb rubbed against the ridge of Bax's cock, sliding nice and slow, tracing each bump.

"Jason. Christ. Feels so damned good." Bax had a strong stance, legs spread wide, hips starting to push up. Every movement telegraphed to him how Bax felt. He didn't have to see it.

He groaned, his cock filling right back up. His Bax. His cowboy. Fuck yes. The very tip of his finger stroked the slit of Bax's cock.

"Fuck!" Bax almost fell against him, making them both slide on the slick tub.

"Good or bad?" He got one hand around Bax's hip.

"Good. Good, babe. More." Those hands clutched at him, pulling him so close the water could barely slide between them.

He straddled Bax's thigh, belly pressed against the warm side. He slid his hand down, circling the base of Bax's dick before heading up, rubbing into the slit again.

"Oh, Christ." His cowboy went crazy for him, pushing against him, and it wasn't slow and easy anymore. Then

Bax got his cock in one hand, squeezing it down against Bax's thigh, and Jason was flying, too.

He lifted his face and Bax's mouth crashed down on his, hard as all get out, sending him to the moon. They moved faster and faster, working to keep their balance, that damned cast clunking against the shower wall. Didn't matter. They were too far gone to feel anything but good. He felt it, all against him, when Bax was fixin' to go.

He was right on, too, Bax crying out for him, like the man was calling for the gate. "Yeah! Yeah, Jase."

"I got you. Come on. Come on and ride." He kept his hand moving, up and down.

"Oh, God." Bax came for him, just boom, cock jerking in his hand.

Damn, that made him feel tall, like he'd ridden a ninety point ride.

"Jase. I need you to, too. Come on." Bax pressed down on his cock, rubbing it on the rough, fuzzy skin of Bax's thigh.

The tip dragged and he bit his tongue, feeling his eyes roll in his head. "Bax..."

His hips snapped and that was all she wrote.

Bang.

"Lord. We might have to go back to bed. Be lazy asses." Laughing, breathless, Bax hung there against him, just holding on.

"Yup. Lay in the bed like princes and nap." His belly growled, good and loud.

"We'd best have some breakfast first, huh? Do we ask Missy or make it ourselves?"

"I don't know. We'll have to see what's in the kitchen." Now that? Was damned funny in that sick, sad sorta way.

"Yeah. How about I see and you nod?" Bax smacked his ass, laughing like the fool he was.

"Butthead. I bet there's cereal." Hell, Missy was a hell of a lady. There might be biscuits.

Chapter Twenty-Five

Bax figured Jase had taken enough time off. They'd had yesterday, with the fucking and the napping, eating dinner with AJ and Missy and Coke. The kids had swarmed all over Jason after supper, playing on him like a jungle gym, and Mini had been just fine.

Hell, when one of the dogs' balls had come right at his face, Jason had slapped it right out of the air. Everyone had held their breath, thinking somehow Mini's sight had come back, but it was an instinctive thing.

"That wasn't no thinkin' thing," Jason had said, smiling a little, shoulders hunching up.

So Bax had gotten Jason up today, gotten him showered and fed, and was leading the man down to AJ's little makeshift arena.

"This ain't no thinking thing, either, Mini. We're just gonna get you on the barrel. Then maybe the mechanical bull."

"I reckon I can work the barrel okay." Mini's lips were tight, but Bax was thinking it was more about the whole walking thing.

"I reckon you can." Grinning, he pulled Jason to a halt, nodding to AJ and Coke. "You boys ready?"

"You know it, son. Missy says she's making borracho chicken for supper, so work up an appetite."

"Oh, I do like that. So do you, huh, Jase?" Bax kept up an easy chatter, waving to Coke to hold that front rope, leading Jase up the little platform.

"Yeah. Yeah." Jason reached out, fingers finding one of the ropes. "Let's do this, huh? I need to know."

"You got it, man." Bax got AJ to steady the barrel, got everyone in place so he could spot. Then he gave Jason a leg up.

It made him a little sick, seeing Jase up there, knowing that this could… No. No, he wasn't going there. Jason Scott was fucking born to ride.

Mini wrapped his hand in the rope handle and wiggled, just like always. "Okay, y'all. Bring it on."

"Start slow, boys," Coke said. "Get the feel, Jason, and then tell us when you're ready to get up to speed."

Then Coke and AJ were pulling, moving that barrel, up and down.

He caught himself staring. Jason's eyes were wide open and staring, but the son of a bitch was moving natural as all get out. Coke looked over at him, offered him a grin. Jason broke right at the waist, hips working, thighs loose and easy. All balance, just like always. They moved faster, Jason correcting and staying up on the bull rope. It wasn't until AJ gave it a hard tug and lost the rhythm that he went off-center.

Bax caught him, holding him on, pushing him back up to center. There was foam and all, but Bax wasn't ready for working on Jason falling yet.

"Thanks, man. How's it look?"

"Looking damned fine." Bax knew Jason couldn't see him grinning, but Goddamn, the man looked good. Fine.

"Yeah? Let's do it again. It's making me a little queasy."

"No shit? Huh." Well, maybe if he did it with his eyes closed, it would him, too. "Okay. Get your hand set."

Jase did, nodding and off they went, moving nice and slow. This ride went worse, Mini overcorrecting and jerking some. Coke tilted his head and sped up, tugging the rope good and hard, and Jason eased right up.

What the hell?

Bax called a halt when Jason started to tilt again, grabbing one too-thin arm and holding on until the barrel stopped. "You still dizzy?"

157

"A little. It's not bad. I'm getting it." Stubborn ass.

"Yeah. Yeah, you are. We're gonna do it one more time. This time we ain't gonna go slow, we'll just take it like a bull right out of the chute." He had a feeling, and he wanted to see.

"You got it." Mini nodded, chin ducked, arm up.

Bax lifted his chin at Coke, who nodded and grinned before starting Jason off hard and fast, AJ whooping and pulling, too. It went just like it should, Jason's body following, moving, head shifting like the man could see.

Goddamn. Give him no time to think, to second guess himself, and Jason was still in the fucking game. Fucking A. Bax reached out and grabbed a rope, pulling hard to the side. He wanted to see how Jason fell now.

Fuck him if Jason didn't correct, meeting the roll and tugging himself upright. Coke countered and Jase went, rolling off and coming up on his feet.

AJ whooped.

"Look at you, boy! You might could do this!"

Mini stopped, grinning like a fool, then stepped toward AJ and tripped, falling flat on his face.

"Shit!" Bax waved AJ off, going to help Jase up. "You gotta watch that, Mini. That thinking."

"Huh?" Jase sat up, wiping his face off.

"Nothing. I say we have a drink and a snack. AJ?"

"Oh, yeah. I got the cooler right here."

"So, I passed the test, huh?"

"You did, son," Coke said, coming up to clap him on the back. "With flying colors."

"Okay. Okay, cool."

AJ came around handing out Cokes. "Shit, man. You damn near looked like a pro."

They all laughed at that one, Jason's face creasing in that famous sharp smile. Bax felt good, all the way down to his bones. They could do this.

And if they couldn't, they could keep Mini fucking busy until he figured something else out.

"You ready for the mechanical bull, man?" Might as well be hung for a wolf instead of a sheep.

"Okay. I'll try it." Mini stood up, reached for his arm. "Lead the way."

"Good man. We can break for lunch after. Missy says she has leftover mac and cheese." Jason would do near anything for mac and cheese of it was homemade.

"Real stuff or the glow in the dark box shit?"

AJ snorted. "Have you ever known my Missy to make shit from a box?"

Coke just shook his head. "Y'all are so spoiled. If you add some Ro-Tel, the boxed stuff ain't half bad."

Jason gagged a little and AJ just looked... flummoxed.

Bax groaned. "Now you've put us all off our feed." He nudged Jason with his elbow. "Still want to try?"

The mechanical bull had a smaller range of movement than the barrel, but it could go a hell of a lot faster.

"Yeah. Yeah, I guess I'd better." Jase grabbed his arm and they walked, Jason's face turned up toward the sun. "You think I'm gonna have to start wearing sunglasses all the time, Bax?"

"No." Sometimes, maybe, but Jason's eyes only did the crazy wandering thing part of the time. There had to be a way to train them. Somehow.

"Cool." He got another one of those smiles. "Sun feels good. Makes a guy want to go fishing."

"We could do that after lunch." Laughing, he leaned close to Jason's ear. "Pray the fish don't bite."

Damn, but he did like that laugh.

It was harder work getting Jason up on the mechanical bull. He'd never noticed how fucking complicated it was.

There were the damned mats, which made it hard as hell to walk. Then you had to get up, and it wasn't basically flat, like a bull. It was all tilty like a bull that was down in the chute.

Jase was growling by the time they got him settled, looking mean as a wet hen. "I don't like this."

"Well, I don't think I would either. I'd forgotten how wicked the thing is. Take a turn on it anyway. Tell us when you're ready."

"You're already up there, son. Quit yer bitchin' and ride."

"Fuck off, Coke." Mini was fixin' to blow.

"You wish."

"Ew!"

When Jason was finally relaxed and laughing, Bax nodded to AJ. "Time to ride, Jase.

"Okay." Jason grabbed his arm, tugged him close. "When this is done, you come get me. Don't let me make an ass outta myself."

"Not ever. I promise." Bax murmured it low before stepping away and motioning for AJ to start it at more than half speed

Jase was on it, body moving easy. At some point early on, Mini closed his eyes, and almost immediately went green as the bull spun.

"Stop!" Bax waved AJ off, staggering in to grab Jase before he fell. "Don't close your eyes, Mini. Try to keep them open."

"Huh?" Jason blinked a little, the sweat popping out on his throat and cheek.

"I said, pry your eyes open. It's when you close them that you start getting sick." Stubborn, beautiful man. If he would just listen

"I didn't know I was. I cain't see nothing. Why should it matter?" Those eyes stayed open, though, didn't they?

"The doc explained how you can see, even if your brain don't know it."

"Yeah. So?" Jase got settled back up, shoulders rolling.

"So what happened a year ago when you'd close your eyes on a plane?" Jason had always had a little vertigo

"Oh..." He got a grin, a nod. Beautiful, stupid man. "Okay. Okay, yeah. I get you, man."

"Cool. Okay, get set and give us a nod when you're ready." Bax stepped back, finding himself ready to give

160

Jason a real critique of his style, just like before the accident.

That pointed chin went up and then it tucked and the bull started. Jason had lost some muscle, and Bax wasn't sure if that mattered or not. Jase was all about the balance, still. He broke at the waist, stayed up on his rope and... Damn.

Those eyes closed and Mini started tilting.

"Goddamn it, Jason! Keep your fucking eyes open." Bax roared it like he would from the rail after tying Jason in.

Jason's eyes popped open and he over-corrected, going over into his hand.

"Damn it."

Coke grinned, nodded. "Not bad, Jason. Not bad."

Bax grinned, too. "Not bad at all. We can work with this." He went to help Jason down, giving Mini a hug.

"It was better than okay. We're gonna have to get you a balance board, I think, but it's incredibly doable." Jesus, he might just bust.

"I... Yeah?" Jase swayed a little. "Bax? Buddy? I need to go have a sit, just you and me, huh?"

"Sure, man. Thanks, guys. Why don't you go poke Missy about lunch?" Bax took Jason's arm, leading him away, knowing their buddies would understand.

Mini leaned for the first few steps, then he seemed to get his bearings a little. "How's the leg?"

"It'll do." Now that Jase'd brought it up, it ached some. He'd not stood around that much in an age.

"I'm ready for the cast to come off. I can't make it feel better as is."

"Soon, huh?"

God. He couldn't wait to have Jason's hands on him, easing the hurt.

"Yeah. Yeah, soon."

Jase nodded, took a big, deep breath.

"I got you, Mini. You know that. Good or bad." Bax copped a feel. "This is good.

"Yeah. I was thinking there was no way."

"Well, you were wrong, huh? Imagine that." It felt as if a

lead weight had been taken off his chest.

"Yeah. Yeah, I just… This is gonna be hard, fooling everybody. Lying. And when they find out, I'll be like a freak."

Bax gave Jason another hard, one-armed hug. "No. I mean, you are a freak, but not because of this.

"Fuck you, man." Jase grinned, shook his head. "I was all ready to… I mean, I was fixin' to give up and now…"

"Now you cain't." *No way. No fucking way.* "Hell, I bet you anything, first time you get in the arena with a bull, you can outrun him, too.

"I'm not ready for that. Let's get your cast off first, huh?"

"Why? You've said more than once that I'm the slowest bull rider alive." They'd wait, though. He wasn't willing to let Jase out there without him.

"Yep. You get down there and stay." Jase's lips went tight all of the sudden.

"What?" Lord, now what was his damned cowboy thinking on? "What is it?

"It ain't nothing. I just… I ain't ever gonna get to see you ride again, Bax. I ain't gonna get to pull your rope no more."

"You'll be there, Mini. Hell, you'll see me in your dreams." Like a fist to the gut, that was, and he glanced around quick before he stopped Jason cold and turned him for a kiss.

Jason grunted and grabbed him hard, kissing him like the world was coming to a fucking end, right then and there. Bax moaned, trying to figure out his arms and legs and shit, almost tipping ass over teakettle. He didn't care a bit, though, he just kissed back.

Jase was fucking pissed—he could see it in the tight lines beside Mini's eyes, taste it in the kiss.

Stroking the back of Jason's neck, Bax leaned his forehead against Mini's and stared into those furious eyes. Even if Jason couldn't see him, he wanted to look right into them. "We'll figure this, Jason. I got your back. You got mine. In all the ways we need, okay?"

"This ain't right. I'm not supposed to be fucking tickled

about riding a fucking barrel. I'm supposed to be getting ready for Michigan and looking at your fine fucking ass."

"Uh-huh. And I'm supposed to be sitting in my own bed in a hotel and watching you and wishing." He wasn't saying it was a good thing—this whole fucking situation sucked. He wasn't sorry about them, though.

"I wouldn't give your ass up, even if I could see again."

"No. Not gonna happen." That had him smiling a little, kissing the corner of Jason's mouth. "That's one thing that ain't gonna go back to the way it was."

"No. We can't close that box back." Mini eased up a little, heart slowing right down.

Bax took a deep breath, patting Jason's back. "You know it. You hungry? Or you want to go test out that shower again?"

"I want some time, just us. Then we'll deal with Missy and them."

"Then come on." Bax put Jason's hand back on his arm, feeling like he'd weathered a mini tornado.

"I'm with you, man. I'm with you." A Mini tornado. Damn. Damn, that was funny.

They were walking fast by the time they got to the guest house, both of them breathing hard. Bax closed the door behind them and turned Jason for another kiss. Fuck, he loved that taste.

"Hungry cowboy. Didn't know you would be." Mini bit his bottom lip, moaning deep in his chest.

He chuckled, low and breathless. "I have untapped depths, babe."

Jase started hooting, working his buckle open. "Unplumbed, even."

"If you're my plumber, I'll happily stare at your butt." Okay, he was getting stupid, but what man wouldn't with those hands on his crotch. Besides, it made Jase laugh harder, just like it was supposed to.

Jason got his cock free, and he managed to hold on while Mini slipped down to kneel.

"Babe. Hot." He couldn't think of any other words. Just heat. Need.

"Uh-huh. Love how you smell." Jason sucked him right in, going to town on his cock like a starving man at a pie supper.

He shouted, his hips trying to go crazy, but he held back enough not to hurt. Lord. He might just explode.

Damn, but Mini was an oral motherfucker, sucking him like a high-dollar Hoover and looking like that's what he'd been made for. All Bax could do was hold on, his fingers rubbing over Jason's hair, down over those sharp cheekbones. That mouth was gonna be the death of him. And fuck if Jase didn't act like he loved it—sucking and licking, tongue moving so fast it made his knees buckle, especially when Jase touched him there at the tip.

"Christ, Jason." Bax forgot what all he said after that, just babbling away.

He'd never seen nothing like that. The new growth of mustache—which Jase hadn't let him shave off, asshole—tickling as those lips moved on his cock, the way the shaft was slick and shiny from Jason's mouth.

Finally he had to close his eyes, the sight enough to draw his sac up, sending him right to the edge. Then Jason got a hold of his balls in strong, thin fingers and rolled them, nudging and pushing them, just enough.

Bax shouted, his whole body lost in the pleasure of it. He came like a ton of bricks, biting his lip hard enough to draw blood. He got his eyes open in time to see Jason swallowing, pulling at his cock, at him. Knees weak as anything, he pulled Jason off so he could slide to the floor, too, that damned cast sticking out, awkward as hell. "I swear to God, Mini. You're gonna kill me."

"Hell of a way to go, cowboy."

"You know it." Scooting over on his butt, he grabbed Jason and pulled the man most of the way up on his lap, kissing Mini's swollen mouth with everything he had.

Jason's cock was hot as a brand in those jeans, sawing on

his thigh.

His fingers felt clumsy as all hell, but Bax got Jason's jeans open, got that prick in his hand. Oh, look at that. He'd done that. Jesus.

"Bax." Jason pushed a little, hands braced against the door so they got some friction.

"Hot, Jase. You're fucking hot." Like to burn him, that cock was so hot. Bax stroked, pushing and pulling, working Jason over good.

Jase started cussing, needing him so bad and, fuck, it was better than just about anything—and it was all for him. A little part of his mind said it would be okay if he never rode again, so long as he had this. Bax let his mouth settle on Jason's neck, his lips sucking hard at the thin skin while he stroked faster. Jason's chin lifted, the skin there soft as all get out. That cock, though? There wasn't a thing soft about it. Murmuring stupid words against Jason's skin, Bax licked and sucked, hand moving faster and faster. He needed this. Needed Jason to come for him.

"Bax. Bax, fuck. I'm fixin' to. I…" Jason bucked, just like he was riding, heat pouring out between them.

"Oh. Oh, Jase. Good." Bax watched, listened to his beautiful man call to him, and felt like they could do this. They could fucking do anything. They sort of clung together, panting.

"Don't let go, Mini."

"I ain't gonna. You'd kick my ass."

"I would. I got a cast. It would hurt you way more than it would me." Laughing, he hugged Jason close, relieved as hell that the first ride was over, and that it had gone well.

It would be an uphill battle, but if Jason would just keep his eyes open, they could handle it.

Together.

Chapter Twenty-Six

"Y'all get out of there and come eat with us!" Missy's voice rang out, cutting through the front room. Jason groaned, running his fingers through his too-long hair and turning the TV up.

God, she was stubborn.

Loud.

Evil.

"Come on, Mini. You know she won't soon shut up." Bax laughed, the sound low, happy. Fine.

"I ain't going to deal with eating with all of them." He just wasn't. Damn it.

"Oh, yes you are. I cooked. Jason and the kids want to see you. They don't care if you can't see. They love you," Missy insisted.

He could fucking hear Missy stomp her foot on the floor, the floorboards creaking like mad.

"Didn't you lock the door, Bax?"

"I thought I did."

Long fingers touched his thigh.

"Come on, man. I bet Missy made something easy to eat, didn't you, darlin'?" Bax sounded like butter wouldn't melt in his mouth.

"Chicken sandwiches and fries, Jason. Ice cream sandwiches for dessert. Come on, Jason. Benji's been crazy to see you again. You know you're his favorite guy."

Oh, Missy wasn't playing fair with that, not even a bit.

There was something fucked up with Benji—some brain thing—and the boy wasn't right. Still, he was sweet as could be and somehow Jason'd become the kid's hero.

"Does he know?"

"Yeah. Yeah, all the other kids explained it to him after that first night. They don't care. You're Jason."

"See, there? Come on." Bax tugged his arm, pulling him up. "You know how I like a crispy chicken."

He nodded, stepping forward. "I just don't…"

"Hey." Missy grabbed his hand, squeezed. "We're family, you big dork. I've seen you so drunk you peed in the bathroom sink."

"Missy!"

Bax burst out laughing. "Hell, yes. When you've seen a man's johnson, you've seen it all. Come on, Mini."

"Oh, don't get all smug, Andy Baxter. I got stories on you, too."

"Be good, Missy, or we'll tell AJ you want another baby."

Missy snorted. "Like you'd have to tell him that to get him wound up. He's the one wants enough to have a whole rodeo team."

"Haven't you heard of overpopulation?"

"Well, someone has to make up for boys like y'all."

"Well, good lord, Missy." He stopped, Bax running right into his ass. "How many kids do you think I could have fathered? You have what? Fourteen? Twenty?"

"We're making up for Coke, too. He's never gonna settle and make little Cokes. Now, come on." Missy grabbed his hand and tucked it in the crook of her elbow, and he caught the scent of fried chicken and baby powder.

"Woman, you're a force of nature." He could hear the kids laughing, hear Coke and AJ teasing and playing.

"I do try."

As soon as they were out in the front room Benji was on him, hugging his legs like to bowl him over.

"Whoa, now, son," Bax said, sorta peeling Benji off. "Let's let Jason get down."

"Yeah, Ben. Yeah. I'll have a sit and you can hang with me."

"Okay." Lord, the kid was always so good-natured, even

if Benji did try to sit in the very same chair Bax was lowering him to.

He settled then his arms were full, Benji jabbering at him, holding on tight. Benji was AJ's first kid and all the guys had tried to make things good for the wee boy. He could smell the food, hear everyone else like a dull roar in the background, but it was Benji who made him feel like it was all okay. Ben just cuddled in, clinging to him and he rubbed the skinny back, humming a little. Sometimes you needed to know you could make it right for someone.

"Y'all ready to have some supper?" Missy asked, the air moving as she set up something next to his chair. "I got you a TV tray, honey."

"Is Ben sleeping?"

"Yeah, he's nodded off. Is he too heavy? I'll get AJ to move him. He's been buzzing since you showed, and you've only seen him the once."

"I can help out," Bax said, pulling up something and sitting next to his knee. If he knew Bax it would be a kitchen chair turned backward and straddled.

"Cool." He thought that he could just let little Benji rest for a while. It eased him, bone deep.

Benji snored a little, making him smile at how the kid just trusted him so easy and good. Next thing he knew, Bax was taking his hand and putting it on the table, talking him through where all the food was.

He could hear the kids, jabbering and laughing, calling Coke 'Poppy'. Missy was singing low and AJ plopped down close by. "You cool, Jason? I can take him."

"Naw, man. He's fine. He's getting big."

"Shit, yes. Hell, they all are. Maybe time for another one."

Bax laughed. "Lord, AJ. Missy might need a break."

"She's good at it, man. Real good. I just want a couple more." AJ sounded love-struck. Weird ass.

"A couple? Damn. You're going to make her old before her time." Jason chuckled, shook his head.

"I already am," Missy said near his right ear. "Here's

some more tea, honey." The clink of ice in a glass sounded oddly loud.

"Tea? Where's my beer?"

Missy snorted, the longish hair at his ear blowing. "If y'all want it later, fine. Now, it's tea or milk."

"Come on, Mini. Eat your sammich before Ben wakes up again and wants to show you his train." Bax put his hand on the plate again, insistent. Demanding bastard.

"Smells good, huh?" He got his fingers around it, trying not to feel like the biggest idiot in the world. He fucking hated this, eating in front of people.

"Tastes fine, too." Of course, Bax knew it. Bax knew everything, and that voice stayed low and steady, one of Bax's hands keeping him from knocking anything off the plate.

Jason let it ease him, knowing Bax was being his eyes. The sandwich was tasty—not too messy, not too hot, but still crispy. The fries were handmade, and Missy could do amazing things with potatoes and salt and pepper.

"Did you say there was ice cream?" Bax asked, when he'd eaten his supper.

"There is. Jimmie, you pull Janie's hair one more time and I will beat your butt. Austin James Gardner, will you talk to your son?"

Damn, he could almost see Missy's eyes.

He heard Coke's deep chuckle. "Austin James. She's got your number."

"Shut up." AJ must have whapped Coke, because he could hear it like a shot.

There was a thump and a squeal, Missy almost landing in his lap, Bax scooting closer. Laughing, Bax helped him move Ben when the kid started muttering. Poor baby. They were getting all rough and shit.

"Shh. You're good." He patted Ben's back. "Y'all be good."

Somewhere the baby started crying and Missy groaned. "Goddamn cowboys."

169

"I'll get it, baby." AJ's big old feet clomped across the floor and Missy went to get the ice cream sandwiches, and all of a sudden it was quiet, just him and Ben and Bax.

"Hey." Fuck, it was weird. Just weird, knowing that this was AJ's house and not being able to get up and go make a pot of coffee or head out to feed or something.

"Hey. How you doin', Mini?" Bax's hand felt good on his knee, warm and firm, anchoring him.

"I'm okay. Want my eyes to work, right now. I keep thinking this has to let up."

"I know." Sighing, Bax squeezed his leg. "I wish it would with all my might, Jase."

"Yeah. Well... Daddy'd say to cowboy up and quit whining, I reckon. I got more than some." He reached out, hand finding Bax's shoulder.

"You know it."

"Jason! Want to see my train?" Ben piped up, awake again just like turning on a light.

"I." Well, shit. Fuck. Just fucking hell. "I sure do, Ben. Like you wouldn't believe."

"Come on!" Benji could focus on shit for hours, so he might as well do it now. Bax got up, helping him to his feet.

"You coming, Candy?" He chuckled at Benji's nickname for Bax, the boy tugging Jason with enough force that he stumbled forward, slamming right into something hard.

"Benji!" Missy came running, he could hear her feet slapping on the ground. "You have to be careful with your Uncle Jason, remember?"

"'m okay." He thought. Fuck.

"M'sorry." Benji's voice rose to a shriek, almost, the poor kid freaking out.

"Hush, now. All y'all. Let Jase get his bearings." Bax didn't snarl or nothin', just quietly eased everyone away, and from the sound of it, held Benji off him. "Candy's got you, kiddo. Now, Jase, that's a big old footstool. Step two to the left."

"Hey. Hey!" He dropped to his knees, something

scratching all up along his back. "Come here, boy, and chill out."

Benji wailed, but the minute the kid landed in his arms he quieted, snuffling a little against his neck. "Sorry, sorry, sorry."

"For what? I got you." He rocked, feeling just about lost. "I'm good. I'm a bull rider like your daddy. You think a little bump hurt me?"

"No." Those little hands patted his cheeks, little soft touches that made him chuckle. "Good Jason."

"That's right. Candy and Poppy are rotten dudes, but me? I'm good, man."

"Rotten Poppy!"

Oh, Lord. Now the kid was bouncing and laughing, calling to Coke. "Rotten Poppy!"

He got to laughing, tickled as hell. He heard Missy's chuckle, heard Coke come rushing to grab Benji up. "I'll show you rotten, pup."

Benji squealed, a good sound this time, and Bax helped him up, easing him on. "We'll look at the train, huh? Then he'll be ready for Poppy there to read him a story."

He nodded. "Then I gotta have some space, buddy. We gotta."

"I hear you. We can escape. You know they won't mind." No. No one would make a fuss. A half hour and they'd admired Benji's train and headed off with their melty ice cream to their little house.

He tried to take a deep breath, the wind almost cool on his face.

"Better, honey?" Bax patted his ass, lingering a little.

"Yeah. Yeah, that was intense, huh?"

"You did good." Moving in, Bax put both arms around him, holding on. "You did."

"You know I cain't be good for much longer, right? I'm going to go wreck something or fight something or scream like a banshee."

"We might get drunk and drown ourselves in the pool."

171

Bax hugged him hard. "You know I can do stupid."

"Yeah, I've seen it. Fuck, I need a beer." He kept running all the shit he'd never be able to do again through his head, over and over.

"Then go get a beer. You know where we are." Letting him go, Bax stepped back, pushing him without a word or a touch.

"Fuck you. I don't know where they are in the fridge." He didn't want to have to search and he didn't want to look like an idiot and he hated that Bax had to push. He stormed into the kitchen, throwing the fridge door open so fast things rattled violently.

"They're on the bottom left." Bax said it quietly, right there behind him. "Jesus, Mini, I'm sorry. I shouldn't poke you so hard."

"Don't." He reached for them, shaking he was so pissed. He got hold of one of the bottles, before he spun around and slammed it into Bax's chest. "Here. I'm going to take a walk."

Somehow.

Jesus.

"No." Bax took the bottle, but it crashed to the floor, exploding across their boots. Bax pulled him right up and kissed him, and that was like an explosion, too.

Jase snarled, body slamming against Bax, tongue pushing into that hot mouth. So fucking mad. That tight body against his felt good, right, even through the damned rage. Bax met him head on, stealing his breath. His fingers dragged down against Bax's chest, fingers snagging against the soft shirt, tugging hard. Bax struggled out of the shirt, letting him have skin, letting him feel. That was what he needed. Heat and skin and want.

He kept them close together, one hand wrapped around Bax's arm, the other was on that tight ass. Moaning for him, Bax pushed back, then forward, rubbing up on him. Looked like someone else liked that as much as he did.

Fuck, yeah. Bax smelled good, even if the smell of the beer

started swelling up around them.

"Come on, Mini. Let's get the hell out of this broken glass and go to bed." It was like Bax could fucking read his mind, dragging him, stumbling and cussing to the bedroom.

"Everything's so fucking different." He got his fingers to working on Bax's buckle.

"I know. I know." Bax tugged at Jason's shirt. "I got you. You know that. Come on..."

"I know." He just couldn't fucking figure why right now. Not that it mattered. Not at all. He pulled his shirt off, dropped it.

"Oh, damn." Bax licked at his neck, hands on his chest, then his belly, fingers pulling at the short hairs.

"Uhn." He went up on tiptoe, cock stiff as all get out. "Jesus, buddy."

"Yeah. That's more like it." Those fingers moved lower, opening his jeans, sliding in to touch his cock. He nodded, spread a little, making an offer. "Jason." Bax's hand closed around him tight, pulling him out, stroking.

"More." He leaned, forehead on Bax's shoulder, teeth scraping a little.

"You got it." Yeah, he got it. Bax pulled at him like he was a bull rope, thumb pushing at the tip of his cock. Goddamn.

This sound pushed out of him, Bax's hand driving him out of his motherfucking mind. When Bax's other hand landed on his ass, then pushed down behind to cup his balls, well, he just went nuts. His hips pushed good and fast, his cock hard enough to pound nails. He moved like he was riding the rankest bull on earth, just fucking flying.

"Come on, Mini. Let it go. Just let it go." Bax growled for him, voice low and deep and needing.

Oh, fuck. That was. Oh. Goddamn. He shot so hard his bones rattled.

"Jesus Christ, you're fucking amazing. Love how you smell."

That might just be the most he'd ever heard Bax say at one time during sex.

173

He stretched and groaned, shivering as Bax rubbed the cum into his sensitive dick.

"So damned hot, babe. I swear, you'd make a dead man rise." The words seemed to brush against his ears like they were real things, and he could feel Bax's smile against his skin, right on his cheek.

"Yeah. You smell too good to be dead."

That got him a deep old belly laugh, Bax's hand tightening around him.

"No. I'm pretty much alive and thumping, Mini."

"Pretty much." He grinned, pushed up into Bax's hand a little. "What can I do for you, cowboy?"

"I... Anything you want, Jason." Hell, as much as Bax liked to be in the driver's seat, that had to be tough to say, but it meant something, that Bax would let him take the lead.

"Lord, talk about a damn embarrassment of riches." He reached out, trying to figure out where they were, exactly. "The bed's behind you?"

"It is. About two feet. Want to hit it?" Bax didn't move away, didn't ease him to the bed, just waited, lips and hands moving slow and easy.

"Yeah. Yeah." He wanted to take some time. Touch and shit.

He levered himself over, moving Bax nice and easy. "When's the cast come off?"

"Two or three days. I kinda need to call."

Bax's hot breath fell on his neck like a blanket.

"You do. I want to touch all of you, you know?" Every fucking inch.

"That's a hell of a motivation."

They turned a little, both of them wiggling out of the rest of their clothes so they were skin to skin.

He nodded and grinned, stretching Bax out and straddling strong thighs. He wanted to just touch, just spend his time exploring and not thinking. Holding his hips, Bax let him touch, let him have whatever he need, that hard cock like a brand against his belly.

Jesus, there was so much he'd never known before. He traced each rib, and feeling the bumps where things had broke, he found little scars. Bax's nipples were tiny and tight—there was a little lip at the top of Andy's bellybutton.

Bax's hip bones were sharper than he would have thought, and that chest wasn't near as hairy as his was. A bad scar bisected one pec, and Jason remembered that one, remembered the name of the bull who'd torn right in under Bax's vest.

Fascinated, he leaned down, tasting the places that he touched, just all caught up in it.

All Bax did was touch him back, murmuring when he hit a really good spot, bucking under him when he brushed hard against Bax's dick. The man was on fire, skin hot and damp.

He spent a minute on Bax's cock, nuzzling and touching, then he moved down. He kissed the soft inner thigh above the cast, stroked the little wrinkledy strip of skin behind Bax's balls, sucked up little bits of skin on Bax's ball sac.

"Christ! Jason. Oh, Jesus." Bax twisted under him, muscles straining. It was like he could feel every one move.

"I got you." He eased Bax's legs open, licking behind those tight, soft as a horse's nose balls. Oh. Oh, damn. That was... Bax was fucking everywhere.

"Okay. Okay. Oh, God."

Lord, Bax sounded like he'd swallowed a frog.

Jase kept licking, kept sliding down, fascinated by the heat, by the way Bax smelled.

"Jason. I swear... I... Oh, damn." Bax rode every touch, body straining under his, showing him how every touch made Bax crazy for him.

"Mmmhmm." His tongue slid over Bax's hole, his cock wanting to drill through the mattress.

Bax cried out, good leg moving restlessly, hands sliding over his shoulders. He could feel Bax's cock, hard as diamonds, and that ass lifted right up to meet him. *Oh. Oh, fuck. Yeah.* He kept licking, nuzzling those heavy balls as his tongue searched for more sounds, more of Bax's need. He got everything he could want, Bax shouting and shaking, skin so hot he could fry a damned egg on it. Well, maybe he wouldn't stop to do that just now.

He got his fingers in on the action, trading them with tongue.

"Jason. Jason, please. I cain't... I don't know. Oh, God." Bax wasn't pulling away, no matter what that fine mouth said. No, sir. His cowboy was riding it.

He just kept on keeping on, licking and loving and letting Bax feel.

Bax finally pulled him up, pulled him back to that thick cock, hands and voice begging him. "Need to, Jase."

"Anything." The smell of his cowboy was driving him out of his fucking mind, the taste when he sucked the heavy cock down even better. Bax lasted maybe three seconds in his mouth, coming hard and deep, filling him up. Lord. He was breathing hard, forehead resting on Bax's belly. Goddamn.

"Mini. I... Oh, fuck. You liked to did me in." Bax petted his head, fingers stroking over his cheeks, his mouth.

He kissed Bax's fingertips, nodding. "That was something."

"It was. I know it don't make it all better, but I'm right here."

"Thank God for small favors, Andy Baxter."

"Yeah. Yeah, thank God for that, buddy."

He stayed a bit, breathing. They could go clean the beer up later, before it ate through the vinyl on the floor.

Chapter Twenty-Seven

The cast came off just about the time Bax was ready to take a chainsaw to it. Maybe a circular saw. Something that would get rid of it. Fast.

His leg looked all weird, too. Skinny and pale, and squashed. And hairy? Christ.

Thank God Jason wouldn't be able to see it. He'd get no end of shit about it as it was.

Bax grinned at Coke, who'd driven him in. "What do you think?"

"That's nasty, Andy, no lie. How's it feel?"

"Like a noodle." Limp and weak as hell. If he'd been planning on going back on tour right away he'd be plumb scared.

"AJ says he's setting up a weight deal in the spare room of y'all's place." Those gray eyes stared over at him. "I figure you can get Jason up on it, too."

Blinking, Bax flushed a little, not thinking about a weight machine at all. He was thinking on getting Jason up, though. "Sure."

Coke's lips twisted, head shaking. "So. I got to go back on tour. You gonna wait till I'm back to get him up on a bull?"

"No. No, I need you here, Coke. We'll get him on a level one bull before you leave. When are you going?" Shit. It shouldn't panic him so much, thinking of doing this without Coke.

"I'm heading out Saturday morning and I'll be gone ten days, then I'll be back."

"Then we'll do it Friday. I should be used to the new center of balance by then." That would give them a few

177

days to put Jason on the barrel again.

"Yeah. He does good, if he keeps his eyes open. I want him practicing walking around the practice arena, too. Trusting his feet."

"Okay." Yeah, they could work on that. They could get him out with some calves in a pen, too, just to work on the bodies brushing up on him.

"How's he doing, mood-wise? He's been damn quiet."

How did he tell Coke that they'd been busy? Damned busy taking advantage of having a locking door and a decent-sized hot water heater?

"Growly. I don't know what to do sometimes, Coke. He just… He's frustrated." And God knew, they couldn't talk for shit. Bax just ended up taking Jason to bed.

"I imagine. I mean, shit. I can't even start to figure how he copes." Coke pulled into a Whataburger, ordered them some food. "I mean, I keep waiting for the big meltdown."

"Shut up. I don't know if we can deal with that right now." Grinning a little, Bax scratched his leg, glad to finally be able to.

Coke snorted, rolling his head a little, or trying to. It was less like rolling and more like watching one of them weird puppet dolls. Damn, that looked sore, some. "When it happens, let Missy deal with it. She's a tough broad."

"You think? She's got all those kids." No way was he gonna question Missy's toughness—he just wondered about her time.

"Well, she knows about temper tantrums, huh? She'll hand him a Popsicle and tell him to grow up."

Asshole.

Teasing, laughing asshole. Bax had to laugh, too. He was gonna miss Coke's solid, steady presence and silly jokes. "You got it, I guess. She's not one for bullshit."

"Can you imagine having to deal with AJ if she was?"

That man was all over her, damn.

"Nope. She's a fine woman, though. Hank says he'd take her in a heartbeat." He probably would too, if he swung

178

that way.

Coke tilted his head, paid for the burgers and handed a Dr. Pepper over. "Lord, that would be something. Hank and Missy'd tie it up."

"Don't even think about it. Somehow AJ will hear just the idea out in the ether, and next time he sees Hank he'll sock him in the nose." Oh, that food smelled good. It was amazing, how dragging around a cast made a man tired.

"Lord, can't you see that? AJ just jumps that poor old boy's ass and Hank not having done a thing."

Although they all knew Hank was a horndog of mammoth proportions.

"Might actually be worth putting a word in with AJ." Grinning, he sucked down part of his drink, leaning back. His leg throbbed like a bitch, too.

Coke chuckled and drove on, warbling with the radio, tuneless as a cricket dunked in moonshine.

Lord love him. Bax closed his eyes and tried not to listen. When he couldn't take no more, he whapped Coke's leg. "What can I do for Mini? To pass the time?"

"Take him fishing? Take him outside? I'm fearing that the hard bits ain't gonna be the riding, Andy. I'm thinking it's gonna be restaurants and cameras and meet and greets and the locker room."

"He's just got to keep those eyes open." And not panic. Panic made Mini's eyes do bad things.

"Yeah. And he's got to learn to look straight ahead or something. I don't know. He'll figure it. He's not stupid."

"No. I know that." Bristling at the idea that he though Mini was a dumbass, he growled a little.

"Lord, what? You're just twitchy. You not get your morning lay or something?"

Oh, he was gonna kick Coke's ass.

"You got room to talk about that, Mister." Sighing, he rolled his head on his neck. "Damn it, Coke, I'm scared."

"I know. Shit, Andy. This was my idea. I'm in it, deep as you or Jase both, and I ain't got sponsors to worry on."

He looked over, surprised to see Coke's cheeks flushed. *Oh.*

Oh, he hadn't thought of that, of how Coke could be putting a whole career on the line.

"Jesus, Coke. I'm..." He stopped. Coke didn't need apologies. That wasn't what the man was about. "Hell, I believe in him, too. Thank you."

"Anytime." Coke tilted his head, pursed his lip. "You reckon they make pool tables for blind folks?"

"I don't know." That was part of the problem. He didn't know what they did do for blind folks, and they couldn't let on that Jase was one for them to do this.

"Me either. We got to find us someone to do research on the computer."

"We do." That wasn't his thing, even if his gnarled up hands were worth a damn for typing, which they weren't, Bax wouldn't know how to use them to surf the web.

"I'll talk to Dillon. He's all technical and shit."

Bax hid a groan. Dillon was a great guy, but he could jabber like nothing going. "He has to know he can't talk on it."

"Andy Baxter, don't you think for a second I'm stupid."

Oh, man. Coke sounded damn near affronted.

"I don't!" He smacked his hand against the dashboard, jostling everything and feeling like a fool for it. "I just don't know what to *do.*"

"Well, I don't either, but Jesus Christ, we got friends, you and me. We got lots of real friends and we got to cowboy up and make this work or admit we can't and put Jason in some fucking state home so they can teach him."

"No. No fucking homes." Bax nodded, his mouth thinning down to a tight line. "We'll do this. I just got to adjust my thinking. More folks will just have to know."

"I'm sorry, Andy. God knows I am, but I don't know how else to do it, 'cept by going to our people."

Bax reached over and patted Coke's leg. "No. No, I just get ornery and protective."

Coke nodded to him, both of them taking a deep breath for a second. "You want to stop at the beer store, get some?"

"Yeah. That sounds good. Something better than that shit AJ keeps."

They both laughed at that. AJ had terrible taste in beer.

"You got it, buddy."

He finished his burger, feeling like he might just make it.

And if he didn't, well, who was he gonna tell? Jason was what mattered right now. They'd just have to suck it up and find their way.

Chapter Twenty-Eight

Okay.

Okay, fifteen steps forward, then turn a sharp left and walk fifty steps and...

Oof.

Fence.

Go him.

Jason got his shirt untangled from the wire and started following the fence toward the gate. They wanted him to get on a bull tomorrow. They wanted him to get out in the arena. If he was going to do that, he needed to go to the barn, to the pasture. See the bulls. Get his hands on some gear.

He managed to find the gate easy enough, spending a good bit on unlocking before he gave up and climbed. Okay. He chewed on his lip, trying to listen, to smell, to remember. The barn. It was close, he knew that.

Something brushed his leg and he jumped, reaching down and connecting with something soft and fuzzy and... Oh, man. Dog drool.

"Hey, Ghost. Aren't you supposed to be sleeping?" He shook his head and headed away from the fence, praying a little that he remembered right. Ghost wandered along with him, bumping his leg every so often, soft panting just sort of drawing him forward. So far, so good.

"Okay, boy. We're hunting the..." He tilted his head, hearing a soft lowing. Fucking A. Go him. "Straight ahead, huh? Don't let me miss it."

He found it, too, with his shoulder, whacking into the barn so hard it spun him around and knocked him on his ass.

Fuck.

Licking his face, Ghost bounded all over him, paws hitting his belly, his thighs. Silly mutt thought it was a game. He sat till he'd caught his breath, then he stood up, reaching for the barn.

Okay. Now. Which way?

He headed the way he was facing, getting around three corners before he found the door, fingers finding the chain, the wire that held it closed.

Goddamn. Look at him.

Barking, Ghost ran off and left him, just about the time the door swung open.

He headed in, the smell of hay and manure and leather and molasses just right. The soft stamping of animals, the sound of his boots sliding across the floor, the creak of old boards…it all sounded like home.

Jason didn't know what he was going to do now that he was here, but he knew it felt right, to be out here. To have made it by himself. He walked down the stalls, fingers trailing along the doors. Soft noses brushed against his fingers, little nibbles telling him someone hoped he'd brought treats. Spoiled beasts. He got the baby carrots out of his pockets, offering them on his palm, keeping his fingers out of the way. Every so often someone would kick the stall, making dust fall on him.

He spent a good while just wandering, touching things, smelling things. He managed not to fall over the rake leaned up against the wall. Really, he figured he was doing damned well. Even if he couldn't remember which way was out.

Okay. He needed to find the arena next, find the chutes, see what it felt like to climb over them.

About the time he found the barn door again, he heard the dog bounding back up to him, panting, tags jingling.

"Hey, Mini. You having a wander?"

Bax. He should've known Bax would show up sooner

rather than later.

"Yeah. Yeah, man. I thought I'd come out, see if I couldn't get used to walking around when it was quiet." He was damned proud of himself, too. He'd managed. "Did I wake you?"

"Oh, I was just rolling over to find someone to get busy with and there wasn't nobody there..."

Bax sounded all casual, but Jason knew that voice too well. Bax had been scared.

"Well, damn. If I'd known." He headed toward Bax's voice, moving careful. "It's weird, it not mattering if it's dark outside or not."

"I bet."

Soon as he got close enough, Bax was touching him, hands sliding up his arms.

"Morning, Jase."

"Morning, cowboy." He smiled, pushed up to get himself a kiss, knowing Bax wouldn't have touched if it wasn't safe.

Bax gave him what he wanted, mouth meeting his, letting him taste. There was a hint of coffee, which meant Bax had worked hard on not panicking and running out after him. He thanked Andy as best he could. God knew it had to suck for Bax, but he had to do what he had to do.

"Mmm. Better." A little of the fear left Andy's voice, replaced with a husky note that promised wickedness. Yeah. One of Bax's hands landed on his ass, squeezing, and it was definitely better.

"Mmmhmm." Fuck, he was happy. Damned happy. He'd done it. Come out and figured shit and yeah. Fucking yeah.

He groaned, backing Bax up and just kissing for all he was worth. Bax's hands slid around the back of his neck, holding on, those hips bumping his. He could feel Bax, hard against him, rubbing on him, and it felt fine. Just fine.

Oh, Hell yes. That got a rhythm going, the kiss turning a little bitey, a little harsh. They turned, the world spinning on him, his back hitting the back of the barn. Bax pushed one too-thin leg between his, pressing up.

184

"Uhn." He was fixin' to just cream his jeans, all of the sudden. "Bax. Bax, damn."

"Yeah, Mini. Christ."

Their bodies smacked together, like to push all the air out of him.

"Come on. Come on, need you." He got Bax's belt tore open, got his fly undone.

"Oh. Oh, yeah." Bax got a hand around them, pulling their cocks together, rubbing like a madman. As if he was putting resin on his glove.

Shit.

That visual had him humping, head thrown back and holding on tight.

"Jase!" Bax shouted out, and that bad leg stuttered against him, Bax's hand pulled at him, and damned if Andy didn't just come. All over.

It would've took a way stronger man than him to hold out, so he didn't. He just gave it up, grunting out Bax's name.

Bax kissed him, so hard it hurt, so hard he could feel every fucking word the man didn't say. Damn.

He rested his forehead against Bax's, swayed. "Mornin'."

"Hey. You hungry?"

That empty belly of Bax's growled hard, making him chuckle.

"You know it, man. I could eat something Beau Lafitte cooked."

"Oh, gross. You remember when he tried to feed you that whole basket of mudbugs?"

"Hell, yes. Grinning like a Goddamn evil fool."

"That was just nasty, Mini. I ain't that hungry." Bax grinned against his mouth, kissing him again. "I could have some bacon, though."

"Mmmhmm. I want some toast and eggs, too." He was figuring out how to use a fork again without seeming like a fool. Soup was still hard, but eggs he could do.

He tugged out his handkerchief, got them cleaned up a little. "Did you see, man? I got out here, found it by myself."

In the dark.

"I did. You did good, Jase. Real good."

One hand stroked the small of his back, Bax staying close, but loose and easy.

He nodded, grinning to beat the band as Bax helped him find the door, Ghost running beside him.

He'd done good.

Chapter Twenty-Nine

Bax went to the bathroom as soon as they got back to the main house, leaving Jason with Coke, who was making pancakes in the shapes of all the kids' names.

He didn't make no noise, didn't have the screaming fit he wanted to have. Bax just stood there with his hands clenched into fists and shook. Like a leaf in a fucking blue norther wind. Jason had scared him near to death when he'd started awake at dawn and Jason was gone.

Taking a deep breath, Bax splashed some water on his face, then flushed the toilet, just in case. Jason had done good and none of the disasters he'd imagined had come to pass. He needed to cowboy up and go out there and be decent.

He ran right into AJ on the way out of the bathroom, whacking his chin against the tall bastard's shoulder. That was when he exploded.

"Goddamn it, AJ, would you fucking watch where you're going?"

"Don't you snarl at me, asshole. I was watching!" AJ puffed right up like a big old frog.

Missy's voice cut through both of them growling. "You watch your mouths, both of you. There are five little ones in this house listening to you!"

His ears got hot, and Bax felt duly chastised. Not sorry, but chastised. Somewhere he had to have a pack of cigarettes. He'd just go out and smoke.

"Sorry, baby." AJ rolled his eyes, offered him a grin. "Sorry, man. It was a fucking long night. Janie's sick with an earache and the baby kept getting woke up. Is it too early for a beer?"

"Yeah." Shaking his head, Bax clapped AJ on the shoulder. "Coke's making pancakes."

"Heaven help us." AJ leaned close. "Man, is it time to get on the road yet? I mean, damn."

"Coke says Saturday." Jesus. He didn't want to think of Coke and AJ leaving, didn't want to do all this with just him and Mini.

"You wanna come? You could room with me. Hell, they'd love to have you at the meet and greet."

"No. No, Aje, I have to stay here." He thought he did good with that, biting back his instinctive rage at how AJ just didn't think.

"Yeah. Missy said you'd say that." AJ clapped his shoulder, grinned. "Y'all oughta take the horses out while we're gone, exercise them."

"I will." That he could do. Riding horses would be good for his leg, and good for Jason's sense of balance. "Come on, let's get some food."

"Yep. If you're lucky, Coke made you a pancake shaped like AWOL or Berry Pickin'. I hear he does a mad Brahma."

"You're a sick man, buddy."

They got to the kitchen just in time to see Coke turn out pancake that looked like a rooster with a giant hard-on.

Good Lord.

Ben and Dalton were flanking Jason, who was sitting at the breakfast table almost asleep, nodding between them.

"What the he-heck is that supposed to be, Coke?" Bax pulled out a chair and grabbed the orange juice, staring at the weird blob of dough.

"Scooby Doo. Cain't you tell?"

"Maybe Jason could."

AJ whapped his head hard, but Missy just cracked up, turning to bury her head in the fridge. Then they all started laughing, even the little ones who couldn't know what the fuck was funny.

Jason perked up a little, eyes moving a little wild, and Bax

188

poured himself some juice. "You get fed yet, Mini?"

"Nah. The kids were first, you know?" Jason grinned at him. "Man, I might need a nap this afternoon."

"You think?" He could so do that. Wake up the right way this time. Of course, he hadn't been invited yet.

"I do."

He got a grin, slow and wicked and just... Damn. Man, that was one hell of an invitation.

"Oh." If he wasn't careful, he'd choke to death. "Cool. Uh. Orange juice?"

"Sure. You want some, Ben? Dalton? Jimmie? Janie?"

Missy looked over. "Jimmie gets the sippy cup, Andy. Half full."

"Nope. We got milk. It makes you strong so you can ride bulls." Dalton was his daddy's son, through and through.

"You just don't want it because it makes your throat hurt, weenie." Janie stuck her tongue out at Dalton before her momma's growl stopped it all.

"I want some." Ben smiled and held out his cup. Lord, that boy had himself a bad case of hero worship. It was something to behold.

He poured half a glass for Ben, half a glass for Jase, both blond heads bobbing in thanks. Then he got the sippy cup filled.

Lord, how all these gals did this all day, every day, with them all out working, he didn't know.

Bax bit back his smile, but he couldn't hold his chuckle when Coke winked at him and slapped a bull shaped pancake down in front of Jason.

"What are they laughing at, Ben? What did Coke make for me?"

"It's a bull, Unca Jason. Like the ones you ride. Can't you see it?"

"No, dummy. Uncle Jason cain't see nothing no more."

They all stared over at Janie a second before Missy snapped her fingers, eyes just flashing.

"Jane Marie Gardner! I don't care if you've been sick. You

189

apologize to your brother right *now* and then you get your butt into your room and think about what you've done!"

"M'sorry." Janie ran off sniffling and Ben stared and Jason looked like he wanted to crawl away.

Bax opened his mouth, but Ben beat him to it. "It's a bull, Unca Jason. With horns. You want maple or molasses?"

"Maple, please. Molasses sticks to my tongue." Jason grinned and leaned toward Ben, bumping shoulders.

Dalton looked over at Jason's plate. "Can I have bull, too, Poppy? I'm gonna ride 'em, you know?"

Coke chuckled, rolled his eyes. "You mean you ain't gonna be a bullfighter like me, son?"

"Daddy says I'm as slow as Uncle Candy, Poppy."

"Oh, Lord." Jason grinned huge. "You'd best hope one of your cousins grows up to be fast like Coke."

"Ha. Ha."

His pancake ended up looking like a penis. Bax stared at it for a minute before glaring at Coke.

Coke looked over at him, just grinning like a horse. "Well, you know what they say…"

"What's that? Never trust a bullfighter outside the arena?" He covered the damned thing with butter and syrup, very deliberately cutting off the head first.

It was worth it, to see both AJ and Coke wince. Missy busied herself getting Jimmie in a high chair with some Cheerios and little Daisy a bottle. That woman was something else. Bax admired her for a minute, just enjoying the way she was so much like Jason's momma. Took tough women to deal with cowboys. The pancakes were surprisingly good, and Bax snorted. "You cook better than Beau, Coke."

"Shit. A blind toothless Yankee with no arms to stir could cook better than Beau. No offense, Jason."

"None taken."

Bax stared for a second or two, then he lost it, laughing until he was bent over double, holding his middle. The baby started to squeal, banging her little hands, making a ruckus.

"Lord have mercy." Missy dumped little Daisy into AJ's arms, laughing along with him, with all of them.

All things considered, Bax figured he'd made it through his first scare with Jason pretty damned well. Hell, give him the nap Jason was promising, and he might just live.

Until the next time.

Chapter Thirty

He'd gone from barrel to mechanical bull to horse. He'd wandered the pasture, worked the arena. Now it was time. Today.

This morning.

He sat on the sofa, thinking. Smoking. Listening to the sounds of shit outside.

"You ready, Mini?"

Bax came and sat next to him, hand landing on his thigh.

"I don't know. I think so, yeah. I mean, it's a level one. I did that fifteen years ago."

"Just keep your eyes open, yeah?"

Bax hijacked his smoke, plucking it out of his fingers.

"Butthead." He reached over, fingers twining with Bax's. "Your leg's okay?"

"It'll do. I have a lot more weights to do, a lot more muscle building."

Yeah, he knew that one all right. It sucked, but it was doable.

He grinned, feeling a little wicked. "You didn't mind working out last night." Man, that weight bench was sturdy.

Coughing, Bax whacked him. "Don't make me choke to death on your smoke, asshole. Last night was somethin' else. I had the best spotter."

Yeah. Yeah, and he'd had one hell of a ride. "I'd do it anytime."

"Not to mention that it works all your riding muscles."

Oh, man, it was gonna be hard to get on a bull if he had a stiffie.

"It does. It's like the perfect core exercise." Up. Down.

Back. Forth.

"It so is. From either side."

A whisper of air was all the warning he got before Bax's mouth landed on his.

Oh, hell yeah. He let Bax push him down on the sofa, trusting the fine son of a bitch to keep him in the middle.

Bax kissed him like a starving man, tongue pushing between his lips, tasting him deep. Now that the cast was off, Bax was a hell of a lot more agile, sliding between his thighs and pushing. Oh, hell yeah. He could have a ride. He wrapped one leg around Bax's hip, holding tight.

"Mini."

Licking a line down his neck, Bax bit him a little, right under his collarbone. Oral bastard.

"Yeah. Yeah. Come on. Got an edge."

"I'm all about sanding off rough edges, Jase."

Bax moved right on down, licking over to one nipple, lips wrapping around it.

Fuck. His eyes flew open, hands landing on Bax's shoulder. "Damn. Damn, I. Bax."

"Mmm."

Still starving. That was his cowboy. Bax sucked hard, making him buck and twist.

It was like his muscles couldn't decide whether to jerk, to go tight or loose. His other nipple got the same treatment, Bax licking and sucking and biting. Those lean hips moved between his legs, Bax humping like crazy.

"Making me bugnuts."

One foot landed on the floor, his hips bucking up.

"Yeah?" Bax's lips moved against his skin, making him shiver. "Wait until I get to sucking you."

"Oh, Jesus." His cock was harder than woodpecker's lips.

"Gonna, Mini." Moving lower, Bax kissed his belly before pushing down his sweats and rubbing one cheek against his cock.

"Oh. Oh, Bax. Cowboy." His breath got all caught up in his throat, his throat gone all dry.

"I got you." Bax licked at him, all careful like, but then just sucked him in, lips closing around him a little too hard. Didn't matter. It still felt like heaven.

He spread all out, groaning, fingers touching Bax's cheeks, chin. They were bristly as hell, because Bax needed to shave, but he didn't care about that either. All he could care about was the feel of Bax's mouth, moving up and down, taking him deep. He did his dead-level best to not move, to let Bax do however, but fuck, it was tough. Bax could read him, though, knew how much he needed more, and gave it to him. One hand came up to cup his balls, pushing them up against the base of his cock, and Bax moved faster, harder.

Words started pouring out of him, letting Bax know how fucking hot it was, how fucking amazing it was. It got better, too, Bax more confident, those teeth tucked under Bax's lips. Before long Bax was going all the way down, lips sealing around the base of his cock.

His hips started rocking, deep sounds pouring out of him. So good. So fucking good. Those hands urged him on, pulling at him, making him rock faster. He could almost see Bax, eyes closed, dark lashes lying on those sharp cheekbones, mouth around his... Yeah. Damn.

He grunted out a warning before he let loose, his balls just aching as he shot. Bax grunted back, but didn't back off none, taking everything he had to give. His cowboy. His.

"I... Damn. Damn, Bax. So good." Man, he had babyhead.

"Not bad at all, Mini. Not bad at all."

Bax sounded hoarse, that voice rough and hot.

Jason tugged Bax up, took that mouth good and hard, thanking his cowboy as best he could. Bax just swarmed over him, moaning, loving on him, hands holding his head in place so the kiss could go deep. Hot.

He got one hand pushed in Bax's sweats, fingers wrapping around the heavy prick, pumping like he was resining up his bull rope. Fuck, yes. Smelled so goddamn good.

"I... Oh. Jase. Please."

Listen to that. Listen to Bax needing him like that. Bax's

fingers clutched against his shoulders, holding them still so Bax could use the leverage.

"Anything. Come on. You smell so fucking good, cowboy."

"Oh, fuck, Jase."

Bax bucked against him, their skin slapping together, and wet heat spilled over his hand. Bax gave it up so perfect.

"Man. Man, you..." He eased his strokes, nuzzling into Bax's throat.

"Mmm. No, you, Mini."

Chuckling, Bax licked at his skin, sounding as relaxed as he felt.

"Yeah." Oh, now. He could get out there now, ride himself a bull or two, just for fun.

"You want some food before we start? Do you smell something burning?"

"Oh, for fuck's sake!" He pulled away, hands searching. "No more cigarettes for you!"

"Well, you started it. Where were you gonna put it out? On your hand?"

Bax moved, too, rustling around, and finally he heard a satisfied grunt.

"Got it. Only burned a little hole in the rug."

"Fuck you." He started chuckling. "There's a lid or something here somewhere."

"Yeah? Oh. Well, then. Food?"

The burning smell faded to a dull roar.

"Yeah. Eggs?" He was learning to do those in the nuker.

"Sure. I'll make some toast."

Wasn't neither one of them a cook, but they tended to avoid AJ and Missy's kitchen in the morning, after those first few days, where the chaos had just got too much for Jason.

Besides, it was good, learning what he could do, how to figure shit.

They got through breakfast without setting anything else on fire, got dressed, and then suddenly it was time to ride.

"You ready, Mini?"

"Yeah. Yeah, cowboy. I am."

Fuck him.

He really was.

ROUGHSTOCK

All he wants is for his
cowboys to be safe.

AND A
Smile

BA TORTUGA

And a Smile

Excerpt

Chapter One

Dillon Walsh wiped sweat off his forehead and slid his hat back on, giving the crowd his little trademark hip roll when he did. It was almost time for the short go, which meant it was almost time to get behind the barrel and stay quiet, for the most part.

That was good. He was freaking tired, a little grumpy and he wanted to kick back and have a beer and let his calf muscles stop cramping. Of course, the short go was when he got to sort of wander and watch Coke work.

That was always a good thing. Really, really good.

There were bullfighters—then there was Coke Pharris, the Fearless One. Wide shoulders, square jaw, big old hands, calves like... Fuck, did anyone on earth have calves like those men? Coke wasn't scared of shit and the man knew those bulls like no one else.

Nate and Fred waved him over to huddle, get pumped up. Dude. Coke touching. Nate Walker clapped one arm over Coke's shoulders, the other dwarfing Fred's skinny ones. Nate towered over the other two, but it was Coke giving direction, Coke calling the shots.

Had been that way since long before he'd joined the tour.

Rumor was it had been since before John and Lefty retired.

His mouth watered a little, and someone squawked over his headset, telling him to dance, to get the crowd pumped up again. The first rider was taking too long to set up.

Pasting on a smile, Dillon cued the music, letting his sore legs warm up with a few seconds of bouncing before going into a full-on Jitterbug routine.

He had to stop mid-step as the chute popped open, Sam Bell sticking like a tick to a dog.

There was something about watching one of the veterans, one of the ninety-point club members. They just sat those bulls like the rookies couldn't imagine, even when they bucked off at six seconds, like Sam did.

Damn it.

Coke grabbed Sam by the collar, hauling him up and out of the way, flinging Sam toward Fred as Nate grabbed one horn, turning Blaze's attention. Look at those bullfighters work. Look at Coke laugh and slap Sam's shoulder. It made his stomach hurt, how beautiful that man was.

It didn't take long—Ronaldo and AJ went down hard, Alan and Rick and Balta stuck. Beau Lafitte, though? Damn.

The whole place went quiet until the ninety-three point five came up on the screen and the confetti went flying.

Dillon trotted over and patted Beau on the back. The little banty-rooster man was on fire this season, now that Jason Scott was out of the running. No doubt about it.

Beau tipped his hat to the crowd and shook Adam Taggart's hand as the safety man rode by, grinning at him and Coke and nodding. "Thanks, y'all."

"Look at you, Cajun!" Coke jogged in place winking at Beau. "This mean you're buying the beer tonight?"

Beau laughed and nodded, waving at Nate, who tossed over his rope. "You know it, *cher*. I owe you a couple from last month, yeah?"

"You bet. We'll all meet at the hotel." Coke winked at him, at Beau, then slapped Nate on the back. "Come on, Nattie. We're up. The young'un's slowing down on us."

The grin Coke gave Nate was self-deprecating as hell. Fred was covering for Cooper Riley and the little Australian was almost like a new puppy, trying desperately to get the big dogs to let him in the pack, play with him.

"Yep. It's hell so be young and full of energy." Nate bounced along next to Coke, shaking out his hands and arms, and Dillon couldn't help but laugh as he made his way back behind the barrel.

God, he loved his job. Even more now that Coke was back from delivering Andy Baxter and Andy Baxter's busted leg to Texas.

The rest of the rides went easy as pie, Beau taking the round and the event, the crowd milling around and heading down for autographs. Coke and Nate leaned together, forehead to forehead, giving thanks, just like every night. Fred wasn't in that circle. None of the others were, either.

Dillon always felt a little dirty, watching that and thinking about anything but prayer. Shaking it off, he headed for their locker room, wanting out of his sweaty costume, looking forward to that beer Beau had mentioned.

Coke had mentioned.

Whatever.

The bullfighters came tumbling in—Nate and Fred running and laughing, Coke chasing them, the man soaking wet. "Gonna kick y'all's butts!"

Nate hooted. "Didn't know that cooler dealie was full, Hoss, honest."

"Liar." Coke pounced, tackling Nate to the ground.

Oh. Oh, good God in Heaven. That was kind of like watching porn, and Dillon turned his back, not joining in like he usually would. He was a little too stiff for that. In certain places.

A noogie later, Nate rolled out from under Coke, leaving the man a little like a turtle on his back. Coke'd been broke so many times there wasn't much bending to speak of. "Dillon, son, gimme a hand."

"Sure." Pasting on the same smile he had for the crowd, Dillon turned and gave Coke his hand, hauling the man to his feet.

"Thanks, son." Coke patted his arm, eyes warm and shining. "You coming to have a beer with us?"

"I'd love to." His grin stretched into something real, Coke always making him feel good. "I was just out there thinking how I needed one."

"Yep, I hear you." Coke's shoulders rolled, the outer shirt coming off, then the vest, exposing a scarred, solid chest covered in a mass of curls.

Dillon nodded, but he wasn't really sure what Coke had even said. He was too busy staring at the little brown nipples. Good God, what on earth was wrong with him tonight? Usually he could be cool if he needed to.

There was this little scar, curling down from Coke's ribcage down into the tighty-whities. *Yum.*

"How's Jason and Andy, man?" Fred still sounded more like Australia than anyone on tour but Packer. Even Adrian said 'y'all' sometimes.

Nate and Coke shared a quick, weird glance, then Coke shrugged. "They're both in rehab. Messy business, huh?"

Something about the little exchange had Dillon forgetting all about the shirtless thing, making his nose twitch like a hound on a trail. He was Jason Scott's biggest fan, and the man had been hit damned hard.

"Real messy," Dillon agreed, giving Coke a look.

Coke's cheeks went pink and Nate stepped in between them, puffing up a bit. Oh. Oh, man. Something was up. Something big.

Everyone knew everyone told Coke everything.
Everything.

More books from
BA Tortuga

Beau is riding like the two-time champ that he is, but nothing is assured in the world of bullriding.

More books from
BA Tortuga

How does Dillon take care of Coke when Coke's destroying himself?

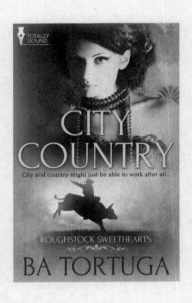

Traditional cowboy Cotton and tattooed Emmy couldn't be more different.

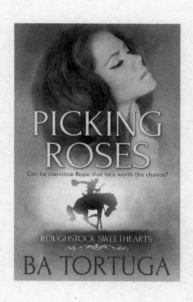

ROUGHSTOCK SWEETHEARTS

Rosie doesn't date cowboys anymore, not since her husband died.

About the Author

BA Tortuga

Texan to the bone and an unrepentant Daddy's Girl, BA spends her days with her basset hounds, getting tattooed, texting her sisters, and eating Mexican food. When she's not doing that, she's writing. She spends her days off watching rodeo, knitting and surfing Pinterest in the name of research. BA's personal saviors include her wife, Julia, her best friend, Sean, and coffee. Lots of good coffee.

BA Tortuga loves to hear from readers. You can find contact information, website details and an author profile page at https://www.pride-publishing.com/